dysfunction junction

short stories by the author of the forthcoming *Dark Eros*

Reginald Martin

introduction by
Darcy O'Brien

First Edition
August 1996

dysfunction junction

short stories by the author of the forthcoming *Dark Eros*

Reginald Martin

The Seymour-Smith Publishing Group
a division of Seymour-Smith, Inc.

Respects and Shout-Outs

Thanks to *The Griot* for allowing me to reprint "Zip Roberts Goes to Hollywood;" thanks to *Yellow Silk* for permission to reprint "The 1st 3 Daze;" thanks to *Obsidian II* for permission to reprint "Post-Moderns/New Federalism;" thanks to *MuleTeeth* for permission to reprint "This Is Not Fiction;" thanks to *The Bluffs Reader* for permission to reprint "May Roses in the South."

And thanks to Ishmael Reed and Francois Camoin for "getting it."

For Claudia who agents like breathing and Tina for breathing.

MENU

Typeface Bombs:

Vidnarratives

Introduction

Reginald Martin's stories ring true to me. More than anything else I have read, they remind me of the stories that fell, in broken pieces, from the lips of women I interviewed in 1993 and '94 for a book of my own, that tells about how a depraved state judge terrorized a town in Tennessee for years, threatening women with the loss of their children and jobs if they did not comply with his sexual demands. These women were lonely, deeply troubled creatures; and they were that long before the judge spotted them with his predator's eyes and sixth sense for the damaged in the human head.

Some of them had drug habits and drank too much. Some had serial bed partners, driven toward one Mr. Wrong after another. One paid up in sexual acts if she lost at pool: "I'm the blow-job queen of Dyer County," she bragged, loathing herself completely. Nearly all of them had childhoods that made Oliver Twist's a paradise. I mean, how would you pursue your dreams after watching your mother hang your little brother from that plum tree in the yard? You'd grow into a rather lonely adult, wouldn't you?

Yet all of these women proved capable of justice at least once in their lives. They rebelled against that evil judge and testified against him, saw him sentenced to twenty-five years. Resumed their lives.

Of course, two years later he was free again, let off by his cronies in a higher court. But he was off the bench. Justice had been done, and undone; justice comes, but does not last long. It's all we have. One can see this clearly in Martin's "This Is Not Fiction;" life is not only sometimes bigger than us: life is also a relentless bully that beats us everyday until we are dead or it is tired.

It is this sense of justice, not in court but in ordinary lives, that hovers above and within Reginald Martin's stories in *Dysfunction Junction*—this sense that, whatever happens, justice does come, for a moment.

Or call it a moment of sweetness. Call it an instant when human spirits commingle, coalesce—then separate again.

The poet Yeats wrote a hundred years ago of the "mysterious instinct" that made him an artist, "that teaches him to discover immortal moods in mortal desires, an undecaying hope in our trivial ambitions, a divine love in sexual passion." No phrases could describe better Reginald Martin and his work, in which trivial desires and sexual passion, both, define the despair and the hope of his characters, his people. Indeed, the title piece of this collection, "Dysfunction Junction," is more likely to invent a new mode of fiction that anything I have seen on the Best Seller lists in the past 10 years. There simply is nothing like it structurally, and the way(s) that it exposes its true intent and its characters inner-most motivations may start a new school of psychiatry.

They happen to be black people, or so-called African-Americans, Negroes, take your pick of definitions. But they cannot be confined or defined by racial or ethnic labels, they are too transcendentally human for that. Which is why I, an undead white male, identify easily with them, men and women alike.

Mr. Martin is as good at portraying women as men, maybe even better—maybe the leap of imagination it takes for him to write about women, often from inside their heads and hearts, takes him where he's never been and creates marvels. But, writing of men or women, of sexual betrayal or of union, of a moment in a post office or a tacky apartment, he gives us those moments, those moods, when after utter solitude and despair and violence, for once, then, there is something, until it vanishes, and everything seems blessed. Call it mood indigo, or mood bright green, name your favorite color, it's there. In that milieu, "May Roses in the South" can be read as both surreal humor about relationships that go too far, and as the most horrifying piece of realism that one is ever likely to read. This imbalance, between the reader's conflicting emotions from "I know these people/I don't want to know these people" to "My god, this is me." is what the structure and dialogue of Martin's writing are so excellent at evoking. One is both repulsed and terrifyingly entertained at the narrative recognition that Martin forces on us.

If there's anything that I dislike about these stories, it's that they're too short. Anyone who knows Reginald Martin's work knows that once you have had it, you always want more. I am reminded of an ointment that used to be sold from coin-drop dispensers in men's toilets. Prolong, I think it was called. Prolong, Mr. Martin, prolong.

— Darcy O'Brien, author of *The Power to Hurt* and Hemingway Book Award
   Winner for *A Way of Life Like any Other*

Typeface Bombs

PREFACE TO MY KIND OF FICTION

1. I have not disrespected the power of the word.

2. I have not ignored semantic bathos and disjunction.

3. I have not absorbed the aped stylistic habits of those in the

   journals or on the "must read" high-lit lists.

4. I have not forsaken artifice for entertainment.

5. I have not forsaken entertainment for artifice.

6. I have not paid any attention to workshop comments—except to learn

   about audience.

7. I have not misjudged my audience.

8. I have not forgotten to respect my audience.

9. I have not neglected to create my audience.

10. My audience has not neglected to create me.

The 1st 3 Daze

The 1st 3 Daze

Friday

. . . that kind of boredom that comes from seeing the world too clearly—you know what I mean. One of those days when your job means nothing to you and you realize that you've got to squeeze some respectable actions and some fun into your little narrative time frame before the only things left of you are the memories your friends and relatives hold.

The leaves turn in Mobile in November, but they don't fall. And when a breeze tumbles in from the south they rustle and tinkle right through February. One of those mornings that you want to leave the coffee shop and pull some of those leaves down to the grass and roll around in them and forget all about the bad stuff that you have no control over and just roll and roll around in the leaves and forget all about going to work at the post office and your co-workers spying on you and blowing their noses. On a day like that it was 7:30 in the morning, she walked into the station and came to my window.

Any action that involved a male stopped in the post office for the ten minutes she was there—much to the irritation of the other females needing assistance. And the funny thing about that few minutes is that everyone knew why all action had stopped—us, the other women in line, the woman herself—but nobody said a word. The men didn't say anything to each other, but she had undone us all and we were enjoying our little personal fantasies to the exclusion, we wanted to think, of everyone else.

It's always on those days when you think you look your worst and when you're feeling your worst, when your mind is on all the things that have recently gone wrong, that some cute guy takes an interest in you. When you're set, all the clothes on right, the makeup on right, your head on right, all you run into are these Mooks looking for you to be their mommy. But when you're worried that your hair looks as dirty as it is, it never fails. Some piece of candy who looks like he just walked out of a suit ad in *Ebony* walks up to you and says all the things you want to believe are true.

Yeah, I saw him standing behind the counter when I came in and I thought, "Uh, that's a good-looking guy." But I wasn't gon say anything to him cause I just wasn't feeling very attractive, and besides, my feelings get hurt too easily if the guy turns out to be married or gay or something. So I just thought I'd go about my business. But I could feel those brown eyes burning me and I didn't want him to stop.

So when she finally got up to be next in line I made sure I was the first one to yell out "Next!" I mean, all those other guys standing around nervous and paralyzed. Umma man, I been told "NO!" so many times that the pain just kinda stings and then it's gone, like a mosquito bite. So when she got to the counter I took her order and when I came back with the postage I said, "You sure do look good this fall morning."

"I look good every morning.

"I know that's right. Could I call you sometimes?"

"We-l-l-l . . . you might better let me call you cause um in an out. What's your number?"

The numbers came out so fast that she had to ask me to repeat them. I was blubbering all over the stamps, the veins in my neck bulging, blood rushing to my head, um dropping stuff all over the place. I told her anytime after six was a good time to call. I knew that would give me time to get my twenty-minute run in at the park and do my chest, shoulders, and triceps on the bench, clean up, and then I could put on my socializing head and be reasonably entertaining. Man, I mean everything just stopped in the post office. The woman was magnetic body from way back. After she swayed out, the whole building exhaled.

But you had to be there that morning to feel all the vibes and goodness I'm talking about that were happening between me and him. Oh my, it was just . . . I think I would have just died if he hadn't said something to me. And I felt him comin. Do you know what I mean? I mean, see, I'm a Buddhist, and I had been keepin up on my chanting pretty good, and lately I had been feeling something very . . . something big and positive was pushing in on my Karmic force field, and I didn't know what or from where, but I knew something was about to go down and it wasn't going to be negative.

Gosh, this guy was just emitting—no, he was shooting all these warm and sexual thoughts all over me, all around my neck, shoulders, torso, legs. And outside it was so bright and everybody seemed to be moving in slow motion. One of these semi-cool breezes was gently coming in from the direction of the beach, pushing paper cups over the asphalt outside. And we were in sync.

I didn't know what to do. He sure couldn't call me cause the kids and I were staying with a girlfriend at the time and I really hadn't worked out at that point how we were going to arrange phone courtesy and stuff, and work was kind of up in the air at the time—I do promotions, y'know—and I really didn't know when I would be in or out.

I kind of just floated around all day. Even the most tiring and degrading aspects of job hunting kind of just got done without me thinking too much about them. I was thinking about that man, honey. And the cool, wet things he said on the phone that night!

When she called that night, man I was in the mix. I wasn't able to run the

conversation in the direction I wanted to, but it turned out even better than I could ever have planned. See, she was a talker. She started taking over the direction of things we were going to talk about, steering the conversation in the directions she wanted it to go.

Oh, I don't know. I guess I've just about had enough sex for 100 people. And I'm talking about state-of-the-art sexo-technics. I mean, people always talkin about "You'll have something to tell your grandkids." Man, I couldn't generate enough kids to have the number of grandkids it would take for me to give each one ofem a piece of my complete tale.

So, I was just thinking for once I'd like to keep my piece in my pocket and have what dull people call "a friend." And she was makin that easy: after about five minutes you could tell that she was somebody that you really wanted to know, to keep around as a friend, cause she was not only sexy and smart in every direction she was a good person way deep inside of her. And even better, I decided that this goodness didn't just happen to be. She had made herself worth knowing, worked on herself and remade herself brand new through enough hard times to drive even Bill Cosby to the Crack House.

Anyway, we talked and talked about her, her life, things she had done, been through. From cheerleader to Black Muslim to Buddhist will take your head in a few different directions, I'll tell you that. I told her all about myself: stumbling out of college with the highest grade average of

anyone majoring in sociology, only to find that the best job I could get would be at the post office as a letter handler; loving to work out with the weights, basketball; learning to read for pleasure again and to really understand what I was reading; hanging out at the museums. I mean, I was as dull as Sunday, and then she said something that—well—

Ooo, that man was fun to talk to on the phone. I was taking over the conversation as usual, but it was like he wanted me to. He was interested in the things I had to say, and he knew things about what my life had been through. I talked about my kids. He told me he didn't have any and why. He liked basketball, anything athletic really. Monster movies. And the man could make you bust out laughing in the middle of a funeral.

He told me this joke—wait, I wanna make sure I get it right. O.K. we were talking about writing and I was telling him that I had kept a very detailed diary for the past fifteen years and he told me that he wrote long letters to his grandmother, poetry, fiction, all the time, cause he just enjoyed doing it. And I asked why he thought there weren't more Black writers on the market, and he said that the best Black writers wrote in the market that paid the most and was the least hostile, which is pop music. Said he knew why, too, but it wasn't the right time or place to get into that. And then he said—oh, it was a riot! He said, "Then again though you know how the public perceives some things. Maybe some writers just aren't interested in giving the market what it seems to want. The miracle ain't that the mule spoke; the miracle was that the mule had even had an inclination to speak in the first place."

Oh, I fell over on the floor laughing! And he was laughing, and the next thing I knew, the words just came out. I really didn't give a damn at that point.

Man, this woman said to me she "really would be interested in finding out what it would be like to make love to me one day soon." You see what I mean? It's just like I was telling you last week every time I try to be cool, what dull people call a "nice guy," they practically violate me. It's in the raw. So I said, "Are you sure that's what you want? I'm a wild man sometimes." And then you know what she said? She said, "I'll tame you." Just like that, with that Sade voice. "I'll tame you." Knocked me to my knees. I couldn't say a word. Then she said. "What do you want to do about disease? There's a lot of it going around." So I told her I'd cover that, and then she started going right down the list of the things she wanted us to do, but it was all in these kind of coded, erotic, mystical euphemisms. When she got through, you coulda hung your clothes out on me to dry. I mean, I was a Harley kickstand, you know what I mean? So I asked her if she kind of just wanted to let this "naturally happen," as the dull people say, or did she have some kind of agenda in mind, and there was this silence on her end of the phone for a minute. And then she said:

—I hear tomorrow is going to be a beautiful day. Hot, a little humidity—

The next thing I knew I was popping *Choose Me* into the video machine and trying harder than I ever had in my life to go to sleep so it could be the next day.

SATURDAY

I was so nervous all morning. You know how it is when it's your first time out with somebody, and plus I had made everything real black and white. In a way this made things a little easier. I didn't have to be stumbling around after the movie or dinner or Trivial Pursuit or whatever waiting for some knucklehead to make the first move. I have a theory about that. Are you listening to me? Well, quit looking at those videos when I'm talking to you. This is important.

See, I think we're going about this all wrong, trying to get the type of men we want, I mean. We sit around, we wait to be asked to do this, we wait to be talked into that; and you know what you get when you wait for guys? You get the Mooks and the losers; you get what's left. And why do we wait around? For decorum, cause that's the way its spozed to be? Cause we're afraid of getting our feelings hurt?

I talked to my brother about this, and Lord knows New Breed knows a little about getting dates. And you know what he told me? He said, "Nobody knows what you want in a lover better than you do. So doesn't it make sense that you should go out and shop for what you want? You gotta look at a guy, talk to him, that way you got more of a chance of getting what you want and not getting whoever happens to be left without a date one night in the mall or something. Getting your feelings hurt? Look, let me tell you something. The first time I got rejected by a girl I wanted to crawl up under my bunk bed and die. Overdose by eating a bunch of G.I. Joe heads. But you can't do that—not if you really want a lover. After a while of being assertive, not only does the pain of being rejected vanish, but you get better at knowing what you want and getting what you want. Ok, say there are five guys who pass your visual test in the lobby of the theater before the play starts. Just before the lights blink, you talk to all five. Three turn out to be Mooks, one is from the dark side of the moon, and the last one is a ten and he smiles when you whisper a certain suggestion in his ear. Did you lose? Did you suffer? Naw, you got what you wanted!" Honey, he's got it down to a science that he's turned into an art. So I just had to say what I did cause this fool was talking about being like "brother and sister" or some such nonsense, and I already got three brothers. I don't need no more.

I finally got the kids off to their father's about two. He was gonna take em to the zoo and they were gonna sleep over at his place. I got to my friend's house about three and we were on our way. Oh! We had so much fun. First we went to this museum and walked around for a couple of hours, and this guy working in the post office knows all about art and everything, right? Can you imagine? And then we went down to _____ and we had fresh shrimp and scrod and oysters with lemon sauce. Honey, that Cabernet had me reeling. And then we drove down to the Gulf and walked around for a long time talking about Karma and special postal delivery rates, talking about my ex-husband and his latest ex-girlfriend, about the curves life throws you even when you're concentrating on the pitch. And then when it got pretty dark and the moon was pretty high, he picked me up and piggybacked me to his Toyota.

Yeah, we got into my car and we went to the museum. Man, it was a gas. I finally got a chance to use all that Western art knowledge, which is a part of all that other unmarketable knowledge I so faithfully committed to memory. But the only reason I got into it was she said she was into whatever I was into.

I told her all about Egyptian art, all about the German, French, British "scholars" running around scraping the dark paint off the figures in the tombs and chipping the Leon Sphinks noses off the statues, saying the pyramids were built by little green peoploids from Mars and all that ridiculous bullshit. Told her about Hogarth and how he drew London for what it was: the downside of Jackson, MS in 18th-century clothes. Showed her how much Voodoo is in the average Blake painting and engraving, told her how Blake's friend stayed up for several nights after Blake's death burning Blake's greatest works cause he thought Blake was crazy, demon possessed. Showed her the African curves in all the antebellum South's furniture. Kept a lookout while she did like I told her and rubbed her fingers over the oils in Three Musicians, and told her Picasso had said over and

over that he didn't know what the critics were talking about, "cubism mir-roring modern, disjointed life and architecture" and all that, "my art is African art." The P-man always said that. Told her how Jacob Lawrence could paint better with his toes than most "great artists" could with their hands. And she was eating this stuff up. And she just made me feel so com-fortable talking about it that I just went on until my stomach started growl-ing.

Well, I'm always fighting a losing battle with myself. I mean, um just weak. The left side of my brain says keep her as the perfect friend and all the time the right side of my brain is the one who told me not to wear underwear in the first place. Like, I had to take her to a seafood restaurant, y'know what I mean? It was the only kind of food my psyche would let me eat. And we had a great time.

I ordered these big boiled shrimp with juice and butter just run-ning off them. And I ordered two liters of wine, even though I don't nor-mally drink, but I figured I was drunk on her anyway by the time we left the museum. And then I ordered two dozen oysters, and we shot lemon juice and hot sauce on them and we fed them to each other. More wine, Burgundy, I think, and then we had halibut and long lobster tails and more wine. Man, I gotta tell you, I had to get out and get some air.

So I drove us down to the shore and let that cool air blow on me for a while. Mercy! The woman just gushes all that stuff that makes you glad you're a man. I got pretty dazed by my hormones and the wine, and I think I just started mumbling about things at the post office and Dr. J. retiring—but you got to understand. Um real high-natured, and when a connection is in my mind, it's real, real hard for me to think about anything else. And she was talking about some heavy stuff, religion, taxes, morticians, something, but I didn't mean to be rude. I just wasn't linear.

And, I don't know. That warm wind blew her scent up to me, and the moon was shining on the ripples. The next thing I knew, she was on my back and I was a stallion.

Sweat, shoulders, knees, toes, eyebrows, lips, navels, sides, mouths, eyes, hair, tongues, fuzz, saliva, backs, hands, noses, nails, butts, eighteen fingers, ears, muscles, eyelids, flesh, stomachs, thighs, collarbones, heads, ankles, necks, teeth, skin, calves, lashes, thumbs, points and conclaves.

Mirrors, Antaeus, angels, bracelets, headboards, pillows, untucked sheets, carpet, knocked-down pictures, sinks, rooms, doorknobs, shower curtains, linoleum, baby oil, "Love Zone" by Billy Ocean, entertainment centers, candles, honey, Ysatis, ice cubes, three burning logs, purple garters, cocoa butter, black bikini briefs, "You Bring Me Joy" by Anita Baker, crumpled drapes, desks, scissors, body paint, a razor, "ENTRY May 4" by Walter Benton, windowsills, bathtubs, shaving cream, sheet burns, Emmanuele in Bangkok (uncut version), stuffed animals, dressers, Queen Anne chairs, white stockings. "Anyone Who Had a Heart" as sung by Luther Vandross real cold Chandon et Moet, and a jar of peanut butter.

A reaffirmation of the innate and absurd yet vitally necessary notion that the world is an O.K. place to live, the willingness to disbelieve all the badness your intelligence and experience have already confirmed are true, "Uh, uh, uh, will you look at that," time slows down, an atomic bomb blast couldn't move the two of you from underneath the quilt by the fireplace, views of the human body that you ain't supposed to see, " I didn't know the loving was gonna be this long," the springtime view at dusk from Philip Michael Thomas's Central Park West condo, Chinese food at midnight with The Wolfman in the 8 mm, "Whatever it is you want me to do, just tell me," "The Beautiful Ones" by Prince, the inability to stop telling about your past and the inability to stop telling the truth, the feeling of not being alone, a $3,500 sound system in the back seat of a chauffeur-driven 669 Mercedes at midnight on the Golden Gate Bridge, Kenya in April, your mother's ham (with pineapples and yams) on Christmas, May rain dripping from the house into a puddle by your open bedroom window, "Ooh, that's a good-looking guy," Aretha singing "Call Me" on a portable CD as you're jogging around Cape Cod, the moon rising over beachfront Miami as seen from a cruise ship, "This is my favorite," Rio at Carnival, and a partridge in pear tree.

SUNDAY

Rewind. More of the same—only better.

Your first breakfast after the first time you've made love to somebody new is always the best breakfast in the world. It's The First Breakfast,

you know, and you're like Adam and Eve and the whole garden is ripe and fresh and sweet. And it doesn't matter what time of day you eat this breakfast—well, you know damn well it's not gon be early cause your morning is filled with NEWNESS and you're gonna hold onto this NEWNESS—this thing that is so right and can't go wrong cause it's NEW—you're gonna hold onto this thing as long as you can and bear-hug every sweat drop out of it until it runs down her legs and you have to lick it off; like pineapple it tastes, a million calories of sheer joy in every micro-ounce to clog your heart, and you lick and lick and lick til it's all gone.

So I got her to breakfast about one that afternoon, and we ordered coffee and started looking over the menu, but she started rubbing up under my knee under the table, and it started me to doing what I was gonna do anyway: replay. Man, you just don't know. I get to the point sometimes where I just don't know what's more fun, the stuff we do, or the way I get to listen to myself talking to her about it, inch by inch, after we're done. It's like, one is the exquisite pleasure of doing, seeing, feeling, but the other is the never-ending pleasure of hearing myself remember, and I never get tired of remembering. And I have such a good memory. And I have so many memories.

Girl, I miss him to this day. He was just . . . I remember we were sitting at the table the third day, and I couldn't keep my hands to myself. I like to touch for a day or so after the fact; makes me believe that what just happened did happen, and it opens up the door for it to happen again. Makes me believe I could live forever.

And then he blew my mind right in the restaurant. He put me into a world where all the brats screaming for more pastries and the Baptist crowd coming in with their orange and lime dresses and gray and blue suits ordering mountains of pancakes couldn't touch me. He went back over the night before and the morning a few hours before like a tape machine. I mean, he didn't leave nothing out. He even added stuff that I knew didn't happen, but I knew must have happened cause they sounded too good not to have happened. He never touched me, but he did stuff to me at that table that must be illegal after five bottles of champagne in the Honeymoon Suite on New Year's Eve in the Las Vegas Hyatt.

When the waitress brought the coffee, he was crying; she asked if he wanted to be moved to a non-smoking section. Then he wiped his eyes and he said, "There's nowhere you can run from this smoke. Everything's on fire." We ate two big bowls of fruit salad and drank some more coffee and then he took me home and we burned down another forest. I don't think I've ever had a better time with anybody in my life than what I had with him for that little minute . . . it was real strange how it ended. But it ended.

Well, I don't think I'll be bumping into anybody like her too soon. She was . . . different . . . refreshing—yeah, that's good word for her, refreshing.

She'd refresh your ass to death if you didn't make her go home. Of all the memories that I rewind and push play on, hers is the one that's always in slow motion with all of Jimi Hendrix's slow songs in the background for the sound track.

We tore up the house until about seven, and then I took a ride back down to the Gulf to watch the moon make the waves worth watching. Man, when that night was black and the moon was so high you had to crank your neck all the way back to look at it, and the light had turned the water and the sand and the rocks all gray, it was an Andrew Wyeth painting. Far as I was concerned, you could have freeze-framed it, blown it up, and hung it on the wall. I never wanted to change that scene. I wanted to keep it just like that.

I could see her silhouette and her sweat reflecting, and I didn't even feel the sand on my back. It was . . .real odd how we knew when it was over. I never have recovered from that. I really have not.

Just before I got out to open her car door, I told her—I told her right then; you have to tell people those kinda things when you're think-ing them cause the worms are gonna eat you when you're dead—I told her,

What I got now and who I'll have later, well, that'll be them. But this dude . . . this dude. I'll haveta keep him in some secret spot for what he was forever, pull him out when I need him, then put him back again, you know what I mean?

Anyway, the fact that she made me love her before she ever touched me, that's . . . that's like winning the California lottery after you already won the Irish sweepstakes, y'know? All wet, hot gravy that you gotta gobble down even after the main course, cause it won't be hot later. I mean, sex with her wasn't stipulative of nothing else: it was what it was, goddammit. I mean, it wasn't for the future, it wasn't for the babies, it wasn't for the house, or because the right phase of the moon was up over that black water. She was on toppa me cause that's what she wanted and that's where she wanted to be for her and for me. So when you get love on toppa all that other important stuff, well . . . the way I see it is, if nothing else ever goes right, if the killer bees get her tomorrow, if they put those reruns of _The Honeymooners_ on every fuckin channel 24-hours a day, if I never see this blue flame in silk again, she gave me a joy for a time that I'll always remember, and that I won't tell you all about cause it's mine. What else do you want outta life except to know that one time when you were in it you were alive?

dysfunction junction

Long had it gestated in each of them this demon to get back at being born, the coming universal wish not to be—except for the intercession of The Others (another fable, not for this tale of unity and lightness never-achieved because of unnecessary self-deceit), but for now a tale of easily believable woe lived at ISDN speeds but to be believed only by those in his circle, and his one friend who understood but could not live for him.

Right there right there in the center of the mix it started, but its antecedents who knew? But for them—for our tale's genesis—start between their legs because one had kids because one had to and for all the wrong reasons. (And I know I know what you're thinking ["Everything starts between the legs."], but my friend in this case only, trust me, it's more complicated than that; it's more human, more natural than that, than that.)

For her, something that would love her selflessly, devotedly, powerlessly—preferably in her own image, but then not getting it as the first nor the second—even in her most horrible self-degradation and intellectual and spiritual laziness; no, for her a boy, and then another boy cause the girl didn't come second but you had to have two in case a train ran over one or the gangs got him or the crack got her so you know how it is that it didn't matter that they couldn't even afford cable (but this before the semi-general concerns about worthiness of parenthood, affording to live as a productive ecounits, etc.) but the LORD will make a way cause He always had before (right?) for those Diasporic Africans whose ancestors had not thrown them-selves off cliffs or succumb to the forces of Manifest Destiny (after all come on now, Carlyle was right, right? Only the Africans could live and multiply among them seem-ingly like yeast or roaches) and anyway one of the two had to be a separate gender cause you needed that for circle completion and to exercise doll-clothing rituals long ago saved on the hard-drive and backed up to optical storage.

And so there it was in pink the 3rd but that was right at the chiasmas where that son-of-a-bitch got tired of the terrestrial sameness of it all, turned on its side with the tv on and her nagging on Sunday about going to service to hear the same preacher who was popping her and her youngest uncle. And so Dad was popping her own sis-ter who had been grabbing at his Johnson for 27 years and now received it with impe-tus emanating vengeance, and you needed that fourth (another boy) so late that he was (it felt like he was) extracted through the nostrils, but it kept that no-good at home paying the bills (the right kinda lover for me) for at least another six years cause he was human too, regardless of what the women's shows said, he from womb not wolf or truck. And then (yes even) that fifth but betrayed by biology and now stuck with only 4 (in birth order, these):

1) an emo-artistic homeboy who would forever betray his own longings because of a lack of discipline and foresight,

2) a genius, who happened to be male , but who also happened to be complete ly different from any emanation seen on the women's shows or on *COPS* and thus doomed to forever assert his selfhood-ed uniqueness in a world

that would never be able to perceive beyond his melanin content and manly bulge,

3) the third an iconoclast without professional training and equipped with a work
   ing womb and clitoris who would punish them all forever and mercilessly for
   co-enabling her, and

4) the fourth caught in the spotlight doing a *Tommy* impression, but talking, hear
   ing and seeing, while listening, understanding and perceiving nothing.

*   *   *

And him, a party to it all cause you had kids cause you had to and that first one cause he had to and it made him a man (his mother had told him so) and it would keep her out of the streets for at least six years cause she was good and that was why he had to make that pussy his never-more-to-roam. And this first one kinda looking almost like him except the eyes being a little more intense and hateful, which made Pop feel good for about six years and this boy being otherwise exactly like him in atti- tude, demeanor, concepts and values, that from the start they distrusted and hated each other with a ferocity that even feminists would have stood in awe of and they repelled each other like the opposite poles that they were the first time either one tried to assert his energy through control, and that was that for Pop cause he could probably kick his first born's ass forever, but a son's blind love for his mother and Big Daddy Time answering more bells than you can count was a double team that even in his best gin and most virile he knew he could only lose to.

And when that second one came he needed a girl to complete the circle (his wife had told him so and so did his testicles), but came out with this weird-ass boy who looked exactly like him but who was so different as to be the child of a Bosnian who had never heard Motown, this boy with the penis of a man and the emotional profile of a human being, crowded out by his school books on the dining room table while his other siblings laughed at and spat on him as they passed and his parents tried to drown out his concentration by blaring *I Love Lucy* as loudly as the volume button would turn right, this boy who forced himself a success until they all turned against him at his weakest and he had to take an alternative route, who understood the world clearer than anyone within a 300 mile radius and who spoke The Words to any and all who would listen and be healed and be not repelled by prophecy in rap and hip-hop lexicon and meter, a child to be punished over and over and over until his own self-knowledge set him free to see, a lonely boy not meant to be so until the amplitude of time drew people to him like Daylillies toward the Sun.

And the third, man that third one, who came not to praise Caesar but to densely populate the house in which he paid all the bills and bust him in front of her mother with his illegitimate children lost for 19 years until the 3rd looked the boy closely in the eyes as she was on top and then neighborhood reports of Dad's waning cocksmanship only underscored and amplified by his own bad luck and ineptitude. The 3rd, who came to force the mother to move out, get an apartment, live with her, put all the credit cards in her name, and then kick the mother out back to the father, but remembering to tell her that she would only continue to love the mother if the mother continued to pay the bills, but the mother balking and the dope boy balking even more, so she accompanied mother and let both parents split the charges, that 3rd little bundle of joy so petite and fine, but cocaine and venom for blood and unrealized and unearned security riding shotgun in her mind.

And the fourth, the fourth, what shall I say but Generation X looking swarthy with a car grandmama buys but not enough foresight to learn how to check the oil—

*   *   *

—and besides, dear reader, this be not his story nor theirs, but mine, alas yes mine, not theirs and not even yours, before The Others were brought forth through the power of the reflective Word, who grew up with the first two and who lived with them and loved them— not as those who fit the description at 6 and 11 instilling fear and loathing via celluloid stereotype even through the suburb's drug stupor, but who knew them as human beings, though black, and who sucked the same urban air and sang from the same hymnal and who were all blessed by St. Nadine on a warm September night in the church basement and who tried to be there through thin but who was abandoned when they were thick and envied when they were thin and didn't know when or how it had all happened to them, who watched them all (except the 2nd) replicate an error when all they really wanted was power and all they really needed was, well you know, —the L word— and a lot of discipline, but the worst laid plans in transitional epochs yield only disaster, and I grow more disappointed—not shocked—by the nanosecond when I only occasionally sleep and in the deep REM phase realize that this is not made for tv two inch high characters clicked off and forgotten through the next dead day at work.

I am one of these characters. This our only episode. And we are live.

May Roses in the South

"There was a line, a line . . . remember a line. And—and I remember I crossed that line. Lord have mercy . . . that line." Walter looked around the kitchen. His blurred reflection metamorphosed in the dull, yellow metal of the refrigerator. "Yeah, yeah. I had to cross that line . . . to keep her." Without turning his torso on the swivel stool, he reached to his right as he stared at his blurred reflection. "Yeah, yeah. You gotta do what works. Ha ha!" His very small, very delicate, yet inordinately strong hands grasped the handle of the carving knife.

"Yeah, yeah. That's what my mother used to call it—no no—`Butcher knife' is what she used to say. It's a `carving knife' now. Things . . . change . . . `funny how time just sl-I-I-I-ps away'." Lately, Walter often sang to himself. The face in the refrigerator was now the face of a man who knew how to please the woman in the bedroom, who, as Walter perceived things, had needed more than the arrangement he had offered. It was only right, then, that he had tried to give her what she needed, what she want-ed. "'Man's desires are limited by his perceptions/None can desire what he has not perceived.'" Lately, Walter often spoke quotations to himself.

"Honey will you come here please?"

The blur moved and turned toward the hallway which led to the bedroom from which Deborah had called, the knife held firmly, lightly, behind its back. It was May 15, 3 p.m.

The unrenovated small brick hotels of downtown Memphis in the late 80's were strangely eerie places. In spring, from one window one might see tremendously tall, half-finished black glass spires and catch a cool, fresh breeze from the Mississippi as it headed toward the Gulf. From another window, one might see 16-year-old boys doing 100% fatal tricks for $20, see the decaying wood and brick remains of various failed projects, and lose one's stomach as the mixture of smells from the alley below and the nearby grain elevator combined to form essences unbreathable.

"There are so many contradictions in life," Walter thought as the hallway ended.

It had started as a game of course. The last three years of the 1970's were a time when the pill was hot, no incurable diseases had yet reared their ugly polyp heads or viral strains, and everyone tried to sexually experience everything all at once that they assumed the previous ten or twelve generations had stupidly avoided. And, then, as is always true, the worst aspects of human personality and fate pushed all alternative lifestyles six feet under, reconfirming once again that even the best were human only. And the states west of the river howled in their beer and Sansabelt slacks, as human beings dropped dead like bees after mating and other human beings locked themselves in their bedrooms forever and stared at the lesions, dreaming about what could have been.

Now in the late 80's at the usual end of theirs or any other relationship based on anything but fun or money, Deborah felt that their new arrangement had been a sensitive response to a fantasy she had voiced one night in early March, a couple of months earlier, after one of their extended love-making sessions. But even the new arrangement was now not enough.

Back in March, they had usually gone to sleep with bodies still tingling. Deborah knew that she satisfied Walter because he had told her so. As he had said, he had "no complaints, only praise." Walter spoke like that after sex. During one of those silken evenings, she had asserted, as she lay there trembling, tingling, looking at the tan color of her body in the moonlight, that it would make her life complete to make love to two men she loved at the same time, one behind her, the other, perhaps, in front.

"Well . . . this is new," Walter said, "I thought you told me that scene was not a turn-on for you."

"I think it would be great" was all she had said.

The very next night Walter had said he had a surprise for her.

"It'll be a joke gift," she had thought. "It'll be one of those sex-gag things." But when Walter approached the bed, he held nothing in his hands. Even more oddly, he was dressed in clothes that she had not seen before. She knew all his clothes after eight years of sharing the same closet with him, and the clothes he wore that night were not among his wardrobe. His light-brown wool pants, brown-striped shirt, and thin, tan tie meshed perfectly with the dark-brown woolen jacket he wore. His brown calfskin Stacey Adams were immaculate.

"I'm Steve," the figure said, "I'm so-o-o glad we finally got this chance to talk. You are so-o-o sexy to me, so much fun. Lemme fix you a big drink."

Deborah assented, trying at the same time to keep herself from laughing. Steve moved to the bottle of Cabernet Walter and Deborah kept in the bedroom closet.

"You're really something, you know that? Tell me all about your past, baby," he said, as he filled a small tumbler to a quarter of its volume.

Deborah, wanting to play along, began to tell Steve facts which he already knew as Walter, and which she felt would be important to any new man interested in her. Steve seemed fascinated with her every experience, his soft chuckle and silent, close-mouthed smile approving every decision she had ever made. When an episode seemed particularly naughty, he only bared his bottom teeth and made a farcical "tsk-tsk" sound by sucking air through his teeth and over his tongue. An hour passed, and Deborah wanted to forget that it was all a game, that she was really talking to Walter. When the truth of the situation came back to her through the Cabernet, she laughed, and she remarked to Steve what a great acting job he was doing. With that he smiled and said he had to go. He asked if he might meet her for dinner some time soon. Deborah said she had a boyfriend.

"Just dinner?" he pled.

"Fine," she giggled, "when?"

"Next week, Friday, about seven at Café Espresso?"

"Fine. Terrific!" she laughed.

Steve shook her hand and said goodnight. A few minutes later Walter came back to bed in his underwear and a green pajama shirt.

"Oh Walter, you're wild!"

"I love you Deborah."

"Let's make love," she said. And while that initial night together was marvelous, Deborah could not help but feel that something was missing.

*   *   *

"I never told you I was monogamous!"

It seemed to Walter that each sentence that Deborah had shouted in the past three weeks, after her initial comment about "the height of fulfillment," had contained that word, "monogamous." This was all it took. He was already so tired.

He had just gotten home, and the by-now-familiar argument had begun again. Tonight he was determined he would settle the issue.

"You knew! You knew right from the beginning! I told you. I said, `Walter, I'm not monogamous. I am not a monogamous person.' Now you're trying to control me."

"I am not trying to control you."

"Yes you are! You are!"

"I'm not trying to control you. And you never said you were not a monogamous person. You said you didn't think of yourself as monogamous, and that you were perfectly happy with our arrangement."

"I-said-I-was-not-monogamous-goddamit," Deborah said. The words came out slowly, like the punches of the tip of an ice-pick going into an already melting block of ice.

"You know, I'll admit I've changed," Walter said. "I have changed, but I do not see the change as negative. When we first began seeing each other, I did not love you in the sense that I understood the meaning of the term love at that time."

"Uh oh. Here we go again. Wait a minute, let me get a couple of packs of cigarettes. I got a feeling this'll take some time." She walked out of the room and came back with a pack of MOREs, one already lit and dangling from her lips.

"What I mean is, I did not start this relationship with love in mind. And what I mean by love is that sort of feeling which occurs in an individual which makes him want to really give of himself to another individual. He wants to be indispensable to his loved one, as she is indispensable to him. There begins to take place a total exchange. They would prefer, always, to be with one another, as opposed to being with others romantically."

Deborah sat still, listening as she looked at the floor and occasionally at Walter. His franticness was apparent to both of them. His voice cracked, and his eyes bulged.

"Now, I did not have to love you. Your companionship—and sex with you—would have been enough. I cared about you, wanted to see you happy, but I did not have to love you." Here Walter's voice faded to a whisper. But you said that you loved me. And remember, I did not tell you that I loved you when you said that because I did not love you then. I was honest. But since you were willing to give so much, and since, certainly, you were likeable and beautiful, I grew to love you. And when you said you loved me, I could only understand love in the sense I have described. Do you see what I mean?"

"Ah . . . yeah," said Deborah.

Walter felt as though something were wrong. He sighed, and leaned on his left arm with his hand half-covering his face. It was his fault. It had to be. He had a system of rationales, but obviously he wasn't being clear. He did not have the oral skills to make her understand. On the river, a police boat siren blared and warned yet another drunken land-captain to stay away from the branches and eddies. Otherwise, deadly silence.

"Just tell me what you want!" said Walter. "I can change anything about myself that you want changed! Tell me what I am doing wrong!"

"Oh Walter, Walter. You haven't done anything wrong. You've just been yourself, and I don't want you to change anything—except to stop being so stubborn. You don't understand, poor baby."

"Please! I do understand! But I could be those other things you want. I can be any-thing." He sobbed, and his fists pounded the nearby kitchen table.

"Oh Walter. Your Steve thing is amusing, but don't let it carry you away. I mean— you don't understand. No one person can be everything to another person." Walter became completely still. The sobbing and the trembling abruptly stopped.

"Look, you knew how I was. You don't run my life. I don't run yours. I'm going to do what I want. That does not mean that we have to break up. That's your hang-up. It's in your hands. I love you," Deborah said.

Walter sat quietly on the stool, his arms folded under his shoulders, looking at the floor. His eyes were clear, his face no longer contorted. Outside, the wisteria assert-ed its small buds in the pouring rain.

*   *   *

Weeks later, in April, the cool air felt good on Deborah's face as she walked along the crowded street to keep her meeting with Robert.

The crowd was reservedly walking to the bars and dance places that shared the small entertainment section in the center of town with the theaters and shops. She was resolute. She felt no guilt—she told herself over and over. "After all," she reassured herself, "I did tell him."

She pushed her way through the crowd quickly, with her small hands acting as opposing wedges. Her long legs, inordinately long for the length of her small torso, were exposed above her knees in one of the new semi-mini skirts that were back in vogue. Both legs, beautifully contoured in her black lace stockings, moved rhythmically, showing off their curves. Her straight back was accentuated by her small, firm breasts. They lay inside the loose beige sweater that meshed wonderfully with the blue skirt. Her face was framed by long, ebon hair, which moved faintly, occasionally stirred by the breeze and her strut.

As she hurried, she thought of Walter. Poor dear. He just didn't understand. It really was not so much the variety she wanted, as it was the idea of non-monogamy that she had to have. But Walter was good. He was the best man she had known. In fact, he was not simply better because her other male contacts had been so poor, but because he was an exceptional human being. "Remarkable" was an adjective she had always used to describe him. She wouldn't have loved him in the first place if he hadn't been "remarkable." That thing he had come up with, the Steve thing, was an example of how remarkable he could be at times.

*   *   *

She had kept her dinner date that Friday in March at Espresso with her new admirer. She was surprised when she went into the restaurant and saw Steve actually sitting there. He was really going to do this thing in public. He had stood immediately when he saw her.

"Oh Deborah! You look hot! I'm so glad you could make it baby."

He pulled her chair for her at the same time that he beckoned to the waiter. It was a large restaurant, almost completely tasteful. In the same clothes he had worn before, his dress did not easily coalesce with the attire of the perfectly clone-like and drab attire of the other people in the restaurant. But in Steve's dissimilarity there seemed a betterness, a stability, which she had no impetus to try to figure out.

"You wanna start with a small drink? What would you like? Anything you want," Steve said reassuringly.

"How about Cabernet?" she asked.

"Great, great. And I'll have a Dewars, waiter, straight up dude. And we'll order later. Thank you."

"Well, tell me a-l-l-l about yourself," he had begun. They stayed, with Deborah doing the talking, and Steve adding small comments of "great," "right on," and "sure," until early evening. He asked if he might see her home. His kindness was so sincere, so unprovokedly protective—and she had been drunk.

"Sure," she said, "I understand. I've had a fantastic time."

He stood, pulled her chair for her, and they walked out.

When they reached the house, Steve opened her door for her, then grasped his left hand tenderly around Deborah's elbow. They walked to the front door, and Deborah began to fumble with her keys in her purse.

"Here, let me get those for you baby." As he took her purse and moved his hand confidently from the left end of the purse to the right, Deborah stared at his face.

"Here they are. L-e-e-e-t's just sl-I-I-I-p these in here for you. Ther-r-r-e. A perfect fit!"

Deborah continued to stare at him.

"It was a gas, Deborah. Maybe we can go out again sometime. You have a good night now, hear?" He extended his hand. She grabbed his wrist.

"Oh Steve, just come in for a few minutes and have a cigarette and a drink with me."

"You think it's alright?"

"Sure, come on in. My boyfriend's not here right now. Besides, it's just a drink. He's not an ape."

They entered, and Steve waited for her to sit and then sat to her left on the living room sofa. Deborah turned on the table lamp, but she was still having difficulty distinguishing Steve's face. The lamp cast a blue light.

"I like you very much, Steve," she said, searching for his eyes, but he did not look at her.

"And I am so into you, Deborah, of course."

She moved closer to him.

"I haven't known a man like you in a very long time."

Then he looked up.

"You know how I feel, Deborah. It's just that—look, if you're saying that you want

. . . excuse me." He laughed as he stood. "Which way is it baby?"

"Around the corner. Sharp right," Deborah said, as she pointed toward the hallway that ran past the bedroom and led to the bathroom.

"Right. Be right back. Don't go anywhere now."

Deborah took a long draw on the brown cigarette. Yes.

Three minutes later, Walter had walked around the corner of the hallway in his wrinkled, green pajama shirt.

"I thought I heard you. Come to bed honey. Why are you sitting here in the dark? What's wrong with this light?"

"I— "

"Come on. Come to bed now. You know I hate sleeping without you."

"I— "

Her legs moved her into the bedroom. Walter was already on his side of the bed curled under the comforter.

("Jesus,") Deborah whispered to herself. ("Jesus—I—this is taking it too far. . . I . . what? I don't get it.") She dropped her clothes on the floor on her side of the bed, and sat cross-legged on the edge for a few seconds, finishing her cigarette, and then fell back on the bed, her head spinning.

("Jesus,") she whispered to herself.

Walter stretched over to her. "I gotta go to the restroom." He kissed her.

"I'll be right back. I love you."

"I love you too Walter," she had moaned. "Jesus," she said loudly after he was already out of the room.

A few minutes later Deborah felt a hand on her breasts. She smiled. The excessive amount of alcohol had put her in a gray zone between drunkenness and nausea, but her desire was still strong from her evening with Steve.

"Ummm Walter," she opened her eyes slightly to the blue light that had been switched on, "That's so-o-o—"

Steve stood over her.

"You knew I'd only be a few minutes." His look was very calm as he held his right hand out flat and rubbed her left breast softly with the palm of his hand until her nipple was aroused and stiffened.

"I-I—"

"I've waited to be inside you for a long time baby, but I had to be sure that it was what you wanted. I only want what you want."

"I-I—" Try as she might, she could not get her thoughts out.

His hand moved lower, descending her stomach.

"It is what you want ain't it baby?"

"Yes! Oh yes!"

"Then I'm going to give it to you."

When she had awakened the next morning, no one lay beside her. Was it Steve who had left for work or was it Walter? Her head throbbed.

* * *

" . . . and so that's just an example of what I mean, you know? I mean, it's been so emotionally draining. At first it was incredible. So new . . . so fulfilling."

As he sat at their restaurant table, Robert had listened attentively as she talked about her relationship with Walter. Deborah now stared at him, anticipating. His comments were always so insightful, so sensitive. He was a poet from the South, and one of only five or six out of, oh, ten million or so, good enough to make money at his craft. When he spoke, Deborah felt as though the world opened before her in clearly-worded answers.

"Who can say why the eye holds the image of desire that it does? Who can say why, at one time, Walter was enough, and then later only became an emanation, a shadowy projection of the whole picture you were trying to splice together? It is especially hard for you, my dear, when one realizes that you do not know the whole you are trying to form and how many men it will require to form it." He laughed softly. She smiled.

"As I see it, you now have a clear obligation to fulfill yourself. It is an obligation that each individual has. I only consider myself lucky that you have made me a part of the whole."

Deborah was also glad she had made Robert "part of the whole" as he put it. She had met him a few weeks after that first night with Steve. Now she recounted that first night with Steve as she sexily rasped the story to Robert.

During the entire act, Steve spoke softly to her, telling her how beautiful her body was and how erotic her movements were as they made love. He asked her favorite position, and so they sat in the middle of the bed, Deborah in his lap and her heels

behind his head. While she moved, and even when she did not, Steve held her tightly by the ass and told her how well she made love and how much she pleased him.

After finishing, she lay back on her elbows in the blue light, the lower half of her
body still resting on Steve's lap. She saw him, silhouetted, resting, staring at her, and
she felt his body to be a part of her own. There was a righteousness, too. The entire
act seemed like some type of reunification. She now reveled in that unity. In the
weeks that followed, an uneven peculiarity of exchange flowed between Walter and
her. They carried on as usual, and she always smiled at him in the mornings after a
night with Steve, but Walter never said a word about the previous night they would
have spent together. Only once, in the morning, had she awakened with Steve's arm
around her, and that was in a hotel room that he had rented the night before.

Meanwhile, Walter lived always, always, right on that line, continually trying to
make the performance great. And the greater the performance got, the more
Deborah forgot about Walter and his needs. Walter was someone she had to put up
with because she really did not know what to do about his problems and his problems were certainly not as important as her problems. Steve was someone who made
her forget she had any problems at all. She began to anticipate the nights Steve would
appear. She grew more and more anxious for him. That was the first change in
Deborah. (She realized that fact now as Robert rubbed the shape of a pyramid on the
back of her hand with his middle finger.) Steve excited her so that she resented his
frequent and lengthy absences. But she could not contact him when he . . . left. He
visited again when he wanted to. The lack of control and anxiousness she felt com-

bined to make her irritable. Yet there was no one to blame, no one at fault for her unfulfilled longing. She had noticed, however, that Steve seemed to come immediately after she and Walter had an argument about the usual subject. Unconsciously, she began to welcome—even treasure—those days when Walter tried to assert himself about her longings for more men. For surely Steve would knock on those evenings, and enter with the same amount of forceful passion that she would have used to squelch Walter's arguments earlier.

And so she had begun to restate her position forcefully, almost every day, on this issue of her wished for, non-monogamous fulfillment. At this point, her second change was complete. And thus, almost every night, Steve began to reappear. That is, for about a month before she had met Robert the aforementioned Steve-evoking-arguments were a daily and nightly routine. Then, for no reason that was apparent to Deborah, at the beginning of April the sequence of events changed.

In the early April Memphis mist so common as the swelter from Dallas chased the last lingering wisps of crispness to New Orleans, Deborah had begun a quarrel with Walter the second he had come in from work. She needed to see Steve that night. It was quite a row, but it ended quickly because Walter became immediately silent after she yelled that he should be less critical and much more sensitive to her needs. After dinner, she expected to see Steve at any moment. But he did not come to dinner. And he never came again.

*   *   *

"You see, time is not so much a river that one sails down to reach something, as the Egyptians and the Ethiopians before them saw it; it is more like a revolving circle of actions. And what a person does to another, more oft than not returns to him. So while you must try to fulfill yourself, you must also remember to consider Walter in the process."

"Oh, Robert, Walter has changed! You have no idea how much!"

"No, Deborah. From what you have told me it is you who have changed, and the effects of that change prohibit you from seeing your altered state. Those effects also prohibit you from seeing Walter's confusion and his love for you."

"But he doesn't give me what I need anymore—and you do."

"Perhaps you love me. And I'm glad if you do. Some need is not being fulfilled if you sought me out, and I am glad I can fill that need. But you must not casually discard Walter. You must be honest with yourself, and for that you need to be alone with yourself. For ` thought without solitude is impossible.'" Robert was, in every way, an anthology happening between slurps.

Deborah stared more into his eyes and said, "Only you would consider him so much. You are so kind, so understanding. Could we go now? I want to be alone with you before I face Walter again. After today . . . I just don't know."

"Whatever you decide I shall support you Deborah."

*   *   *

She had met Robert at the beginning of April, right after Steve stopped coming. Big cypresses bent down with rain in Riverside Park as the yellow jonquils—interrupted by fragments of wild red roses—took over the east bluff. She had not seen

Steve in a week. Walter only irritated her more and more. He certainly had tried to reconcile things. She felt that she had tried too. But try as they might they could not negotiate a non-aggression pact that would allow her to be in any way satisfied with his existence.

So it was then that during those last few days of March she stormed out of the house, shouting in front of her as she went, "I'm gonna find somebody right now! Maybe two! Do you hear? Right now!" After she slammed the door behind her, she saw his pitiful little face peeking out of the curtain as she sped out of the driveway with the car in reverse. She had not found anyone that day—oh, not because she could not, but because she was too angry and confused to look for anyone. She had actually stopped the car in Confederate Park and sat, thinking of Walter.

She wanted Walter to be happy. He had always been so kind to her, never let her down when she needed comfort, love, money. But she had chosen to attain something which hurt him, offended him, scared him. But she had to do what she wanted. It was an impossible situation. A few days later as she was sitting in her favorite bar, Le Chardonnéy, alone, after another scene with Walter, she met Robert. He simply walked up to her and told her she was beautiful and asked if he might sit down. She had only heard about a million better lines than that, but none of them had ever been said with those Delta vowels shaped in Natchez.

He was an older man. He had startling hazel eyes and an air of accomplishment. His beard, not totally gray, as was his hair, was streaked beautifully with those colorful parallel flecks of darkness and lightness. After she had said "Yes," he began to talk of whom he was and the remarkable impression she had made on him when he had first seen her at her table. He was a poet and a poetry teacher, now retired. He had even had a book of poems published once. Deborah said nothing until he told her that he sensed something was troubling her greatly, whereupon, she began to cry.

After their first meeting, she met Robert almost each evening. She was amazed and enthralled by his insight into . . . well, everything. She told him as much as she wanted to about her domestic situation, and he was always kind to her and to Walter in his comments, comments that never gave the answer to the problem, exactly, but that always suggested a number of mature, possible solutions to pursue. Deborah became enchanted by his lack of baseness. After three days, she had asked to sleep with him. His love-making was quick, but tender.

May came. Robert's kindness and sensitivity sent Deborah running to him on the day he had counseled her against being too harsh and rash with Walter.

*   *   *

That day had begun with a typical argument—typical of the second stage of arguments that Deborah and Walter had most recently been having, during which Walter always said little. It did not continue—or end—typically.

"I just can't stand it anymore. If you would just consider what I am saying—"

"I have considered it Deborah!" Walter had been sitting at the kitchen table, staring at its top, as Deborah made them both hot chocolate. His first statement was shouted, and it startled her.

"Don't shout at me!"

"Listen Deborah, I have taken all I'm going to take from you. Who you—I mean, whom do you think you are in all your self-righteousness? Have you considered one word I have mumbled for the past two-and-a-half-months? Hell no! And are you going to listen? Hell no Hell no!" Walter was standing now.

"Don't shout at me Walter!" Deborah turned to face him. "Don't shout at me and sit down you 4-dollars-and-40-cents-an-hour-making-son-of-a-bitch-you!"!

"What are you doing? What are you doing? You are threatening me! I have tried to be rational, nonemotional. But it ain't—hasn't worked. How ridiculous. It is my emotions which are involved here. If you knew—do you know what I've tried—" Walter sobbed. "If I could only—I know how you feel about what happened with your mother, but baby, I could never hurt you like that."

"Sit down Walter!" Deborah screamed. "SIT DOWN! No goddamit, don't sit down. Get out! My—my mother has nothing to do with anything. She was a—my-mother-has-nothing-to-do-with-it. You're a goddamed child. If you don't have your way, you break down. And you and your silly, childish games. That Steve thing. What the hell was that? Do you know how weird that whole thing was? I hated it! I only went along with it to humor your crazy, pathetic ass. I thought we could make a trade. But no, you're too selfish. I'm getting out of here. And by the way, do you know where I'm going now baby? I'm going where I've been going for over a month. I'm going to someone Walter. Oh yeah, he's been coming here too. Yes. Ha! Right here, while you were at work baby! And I am going to fuck him tonight Walter, just like we've done a thousand times, and I-am-going-to-love-it!"

Walter sat down.

"I'll be back tomorrow to pick up my stuff." She walked out of the house. For hours, she wasn't able to reach Robert at the number he had given her.

It was May 14.

* * *

She returned from a motel that next morning. Robert said he would meet her after she got to the apartment. Deborah went about the house, putting things in suitcases, plastic bags, anything she could find that would hold small items. Walter came in at 2 p.m., a little early for him to be getting home from work, actually. He went straight to the kitchen and sat on the stool, staring at the refrigerator. She saw him sitting there as she walked through the living room to pick up small items.

After she was sure she had picked up everything that belonged to her out of the other four rooms, she returned to their bedroom to put all her things away. She wanted everything packaged and ready to be put outside before she spoke to Walter. That way, Robert could just throw the stuff in his car. She was sure it would be a bad ending, and she wanted to be ready to leave when she began it. Looking around, she saw that everything was put away. It was 3 o'clock. She sat on the dresser and called to Walter.

* * *

Walter stood inside the rectangle formed by the frame of the doorway above the floor. He held both hands behind his back. His shoulders were rounded. Deborah's mouth fell open. He had put on Steve's clothes. Then she spoke.

"Honey, I am leaving you, but I want us to part as best we can. Honey, I'm sorry I'm sorry you couldn't see your way to share me with other people. I just—I need to know I can do that, have that freedom. Do you know what I mean?"

Walter nodded his head up and down. Deborah could see water beginning to fill his eyes. She began to walk toward him.

"Now honey, don't. I don't know what the future holds for us. Just put yourself more into your work until the hurt leaves. I'm going to miss you too, believe me, and that's what I'm going to do. Maybe we ca—"

She stopped.

Walter had drawn the knife from behind his back and held it at the end of his fully extended right arm that was now horizontal to the floor, with the knife's blade pointed toward the ceiling, the handle held firmly in a fist.

"Oh shit! Walter, my God!" Deborah now spoke in a barely audible rasp. "What on earth are you going to do? Put that knife back in the drawer you fool!"

"There ain't no work to ` put myself into' baby. That shit is dead and gone. I ain't been to work for over a week, and I'm sure I don't have a gig now." Walter's voice faded in and out, but it was forceful in its fluctuations.

"I have tried—tried very hard. You—you have to put yourself into existence. You must act. You got to move and groove. Evil grows where there is inactivity. I ha—have tried to show-you-my-love. I could have been any—anything you wanted. It was you I wa-wanted."

"Walter, please don't. Please put down that knife. My God. Please don't hurt me."

"One must act. I must . . . perform, put on a show for your dumb ass."

Walter extended his left arm horizontal to the floor, and in his left hand he grasped something so tightly that Deborah could not see what it was.

"Wal . . . ter?"

"I understand your actions. Yea, I know what's up, what's going down. Yes, yes. You think I don't know about your backdoor poet? Sonofabitch couldn't write out a check. Ha! 'Why cannot the ear be closed to its own destruction?/or the glistening eye to the poison of a smile?' I mean, that's what I wanna goddamit know."

"Walter!"

He jerked his right arm into an arc and plunged the knife to the hilt into the top of his head. When the knees collapsed, the body shook for a very few seconds, the left hand cramping around the object it held and jutting toward the knee of those perfectly pressed brown pants.

Deborah screamed all the breath from her lungs. She took four running steps toward the front door and stopped, backed up, sat back on the dresser, and stared at Walter. The details were starkly contrasted by the white tile floor and animated by a slowing tracing black outline, in the middle of which stared Robert's plasticene gray face that lay crumpled over the knee of Steve's brown pants.

Outside, into their own red reflections, the intersticed May roses bloomed and catapulted through the wild yellow jonquils down the bluff and into the rushing white caps of irresistible grayness.

Post-Moderns/New Federalism

"Look, all I'm saying is you didn't have to do it. There were other ways of getting over."

Lewis strained to look at the print on the floor tile. He had been looking at the tile blocks for over two hours—ever since he had gotten home at 3:30 from his giblet-slinging job at the Chicken Coop where he worked the day shift from seven to three. Intermittently, while sitting in the understuffed chair he had saved from his father's furniture, he had looked at Ramshan, his wife, as she sat to his right on the plastic-covered love-seat.

Everyone and everything was covered with the sweat that goes along with being in New Orleans even in early June. Royal Street stank below their dilapidated apartment, and occasionally Lewis thought about his childhood dreams of living on St. Charles Avenue. But only occasionally.

The room in which Lewis and Ramshan sat could not exactly be called a living room. There were three rooms to this apartment with the one window to the south. The room in which they sat and where the love-seat, chair, and coffee table rested was the front room. The room partitioned by a thin wall of sheet rock was the back-room. In it were two full-sized mattresses placed side by side, with a king-size, thinner, one-piece mattress resting on top of them. The two full-sized mattresses rested on the floor. Beside the bed were a Sony Digimatic LifeTime electric clock and an immense ashtray. It was bright orange and made of high-school-shop plaster. It had neatly edged indentations for thirty cigarettes, and it was filled with ashes and butts. The 4 x 8 kitchen lay to the immediate south upon entering the rooms.

Because one of its three legs was shorter than the other two, the love-seat would tilt as Ramshan sighed and rocked. She hadn't had much success in convincing Lewis that what she had done she had done because she loved him.

"Lewis baby, you said we would need the money. You're right too. We do need the money if we're going see the thing through. What were you going to do? Take another job? You already working seven to three at that chicken shack. Then you just come in here long enough to change your shirt so you can walk over to that market and unload trucks. Most times you don't get in til two in the morning. And working on weekends too! You were going to have to knock me down to get through that door if you thought you were going to take on more work." She spoke more softly.

"Baby, ain't nothing changed. Look at me. It's still me."

Lewis did not look at her.

She reached into her bra.

"And look at this. You know how long it would take both of us to make that?" She spread the new bills out on the old coffee table in a neat semi-circle.

Ramshan paused for a moment and, then, staring at the new bills, spoke even more softly.

"I just told the old fool to go to the bank and he did. He went right on . . ."

Lewis put his right hand to his forehead and again began staring at the tiles waiting for the next brigade of vermin. He shouted.

"Will you shut up? Will you just shut up!?" And, then, imitating her, "'It's still me.' she says—" Ramshan leaned back on the sofa as Sherman came bursting into the front room.

Sherman ran into the kitchen, took a piece of bread from its package, left the package undone, and ran back out onto Royal. He was three years old, and he was the only child of Lewis and Ramshan.

Lewis put his head into both his hands and said nothing else. Ramshan moved from the love-seat to sit in his lap. She held him around the shoulders and spoke into his ear.

"Why you want to go and yell at me? Why you want to do that Lewis baby? Don't you know mama don't love nobody but you? Mama don't feel nothing for nobody like she feels for you. Don't you know that?" She pushed closer into him and kissed his ear.

Lewis said nothing, made no reaction, except to keep staring at the tiles.

"Now look, asshole," Ramshan said, "don't pull this silent stuff on me. You got to just swallow hard. We're poor and all that means. Are you listening to me?"

Ramshan slapped Lewis hard on his right cheek.

"You talk to me! You talk to me right now! You make me feel like dirt. Look at that money. Look at it! I earned that. I got that for us and Sherman." She picked up the money and slammed it into his face.

"See, see, see!" she screamed, as the bills hit Lewis' face and fell to the floor. She began to cry and sank to the floor holding onto Lewis' legs. Except to blink when the bills hit his face, Lewis didn't move; he continued to stare at the tile. Sherman came in for another piece of bread. As he passed by his parents on his way out the door he paused and smiled, "Daddy, did you hit mama?"

"No, daddy didn't hit me baby. I'm crying cause I'm so happy. See all this money mama made today?"

"Oh," Sherman said, "Ok." As he ran back out the door to play in the middle of the street with his friends, Iowa tourists saw the black urchins on the corner of Royal and Canal and gripped their wallets and purses tighter. Ramshan stared at the scene through the window. She jerked her head toward Lewis.

"You see that, jerk?" Ramshan said, still crying. "My son approves of this money."

*　　　*　　　*

In the beginning near what is now present day Kisumu, Kenya, there were two people in the world, and they got bored with each other and, consequently, lonely. They wished there were other creatures around similar to them to fill up their empty lives. The 2 had talked and decided that if THEY had appeared in the world, there must be a way to make others appear.

To make new people, the 2 tried chanting, conjuring, and prayer. No new people came.

Later they set their best fruit in a clearing under a full moon, but no new people appeared.

Finally, the 2 fasted for several days and sacrificed a monkey to the blueness of the sky. Still, no new people came. The last night of the fast, the 2 went to their cave utterly disgusted and defeated. They decided to commit double suicide the next morning. In their grief on their last night, they wept and hugged closely, and eventually went to sleep late into the night.

At sunrise, they both awoke to screaming. They sat up, and between them lay two babies.

The 2 were overwhelmed with their good fortune. One was sure that the fasting had pleased the blueness; the other was sure that the sacrifice of the monkey had brought the new people, because one had to give a life-form back to the cosmos to request a new one that one preferred more.

At the end of the week, the two new people were fully grown, and the 2 conversed and played with them constantly. The original people and the new people were all very happy, and boredom and loneliness were unknown in the world during that time.

At the end of two weeks, the progenitors of the new people said to them, "You must go out into the world now and be a man; make us proud of your courageousness and honor." And to the other they said, "You must go out into the world now and be a woman. Make us proud of your beauty, intellect, and virtuousness." And the new people smiled and left.

Asar and Aset, for such were the names of the two new people, journeyed to Miami.

It was soon made obvious to them that they were unemployable.

They had no skills the market valued, their inner beauty only an unnoticed, ethereal surplus, a crippling handicap around those who understood only terror and terrorism as a way of life. But with their external beauty, they were soon able to begin to forge their way in the city.

By sleeping with various burned-out members of the grey and unwashed faculty (for such was the only way to get an academic job in those terrible days), they both became graduate assistants in the English Department at the University of Miami. Occasionally, there would be enough money left over from their $450 per month checks after bills to see a show. The following 29 days would be awful, Hell on acid. Both Asar and Aset were raped several times on the mass transit. Asar developed a devastating case of AIDS, and Aset got a habit. They committed suicide together on a beautiful Spring morning two years after leaving the 2. The birds were singing, cool breezes blew in from the Atlantic over turquoise waves.

*   *   *

Lewis leaned back in his chair.   "Let me tell you something Ramshan. I don't care what I had to do, I would have gotten the money a better way. I could have done-something. I feel fine."

"Will you spare me? Yeah, you feel fine. I'm surprised we even came up with a reason to need the money in the first place."

"Well, damn, somebody musta opened the refrigerator in here. It's like the Arctic all of a sudden."

"Yeah. It is ain't it. Sorry."

"Look Ramshan, when we got into this venture, we both told each other it was going to be hard. We both knew we would have to make sacrifices. We both were willing to do it cause we were so much in love. You remember those days don't you? We're not unique. Other people make it and don't compromise—"

"—Who!? Name one goddamit!"

"A lot of people. It's always been done in the past."

"Those were different times. Different people."

"There is in each of us—"

"Oh God. Here we go with that bookshit again."

"You know Ramshan, I didn't cut you off, and I let you hit me with the money without me throwing you out the window. What else I gotta do to make you let me talk? You used to get wet cause I knew `bookshit'. Now all you get is mad and jealous. Anyway, there's something in all of us that gives us the power to do the honorable or dishonorable thing. But it's like Jean-Paul wrote, nobody can make you do anything that you think is wrong. No situation can make you compromise your sense of honor. You have a choice, a will, whatever the Hell you wanna call it."

Lewis began to cry. "It was my honor too you were selling you know? Mine too."

Sherman ran in and out for another piece of bread. Ramshan watched him run out the door, and then she spoke quietly.

"So what do you want me to do? Give the money back? I think that would be pretty stupid."

"Yeah it would look pretty stupid . . . now," Lewis said, still crying.

"Well what do you want me to do? We need to make some kind of decision this week or we won't have much of an option."

"How much is it gonna cost? Did you talk to your sister?"

"Yeah. Over half of it. It's gone up you know. People ain't so willing no more."

"Goddamit do it. Do it! Just do it, and take the money that's left over and buy Sherman a one-way-bus ticket to your mama's in Lafayette. If there's anything left, buy some of that wine we had that night at the student union when we met—you remember. Do it. And then come home. I'll be waiting for you."

"Right babe."

Ramshan leaned her head against Lewis' right knee, stared out the window, and conjured yellow magnolia blooms, already so fecund and yellow in June.

Flux

The ineluctable memories of silken touches:

"The problem is not that one has the self-destructive desire to keep falling in love with the same type of destructive, doomed people . . ."

Eddie leaned closer to the mirror. He stared behind him at the unmade bed. His kiss left a distinct oval and mist. He drew an L in the mist.

*   *   *

The human inability to make the word flesh:

"Problem is the angle was a part of what you loved in the first place."

*   *   *

The persistence of desire:

Eddie wiped the mirror clean with his palm. His naked black back pressed down against the perfumed and flowered sheets of his single bed.

*   *   *

A long draw on a Camel and Edward Hopper's SUNDAY MORNING near the window that looked out on the Mississippi.

Zip Roberts Goes to Hollywood to Touch Every Female Dancer on <u>Soul Train</u> and While There Discovers A Cure for Sickle-Cell Anemia

"Oh God! Oh no! She's not going to squat again, is she? Oh baby, do it yeah! Oh yes, yes. Sing it, Raymond, sing it! '. . . *Tonight don't leave it up to no one else/lock the door and take control of yourself. . .*' Oh baby, oh mama, I say shake it but don't break it. She is so TALL. Oh! There she goes again down-n-n, and that wiggle at the bottom. Yeah! Kick. Now look at me baby, Here I am, right here in Omaha. Just shake, don't ask me what I'm doing here cause I don't know either. Look at that caramel skin. God didn't make that from no rib. That's pure lo-cal Angel cake. Oh yes . . . YES . . ."

The truth was that Zip Roberts knew *exactly* what he was doing in Omaha, Nebraska, as his favorite *Soul Train* dancer stopped dipping just to turn her back to the camera and let everyone know, especially Zip, that she was born in those pants and they had just kind of stre-e-etched as she grew.

"Oh! Oh! Um not gonna make it! Um not gonna make it! Mama kiss your baby goodbye cause his heart stopped two dips and a grind ago. OH! Oh no, here comes the one with the hair!"

Yes. He knew exactly what he was doing there. He'd been a top-grade science student in Madame Marie Laveau High School in New Orleans, perfectly content to study superficially and make A's on the science exams, then rush to watch the video cassettes of *Soul Train* his sister had been taping for him for months on her boyfriend's 8mm.

Then the accident happened. And now here he was in Omaha spending $50 a month for cable so he could see *Soul Train* three times on Saturday nights on channel 62.

"Uh huh. See, she loves to just strut and pose. Now here comes the hair. Whoo! That's it baby, just throw it up and strut. God take me now, please. Just let her be my angel!"

It was an accident the way Zip saw it. It was almost 3 p.m. one spring afternoon of his senior year at Madame Laveau's, and Zip was conducting a simple centrifuge separation of urea. "I just wanted to skim off some of the heavy water, put the rest of the urea in a test tube, cork it, and run home to the 8mm," he'd told the reporters that evening from the *Biscayne*. Later he had said the same thing to the hundreds of company chemists and recruiters from university medical schools. He'd even written it in red ink on his "Statement of Purpose" sheet on the college applications that his mother had made him fill out. All to no avail, of course. He was obviously a genius, and social penance had to be paid before he would be allowed to simply make A's and drool over **The TALL One with the Pants and the Caramel Skin** again.

He had stopped the centrifuge, taken the plastic cover off of one of the disposable hypodermics, extracted the refined urea out of the centrifuge, and injected in into the sample sickle-cell culture that had been brought into the bio-lab that day. It was just something that had crossed his mind the previous night while **Total Bottom** was dancing to "Burn Rubber on Me" by the Gap Band. Urea, containing, as it does, an inordinate number of oxygen molecules that, like other gasses in the VIa group of elements, tend to intimately fuse themselves to more inert molecular matter, such as red blood cells, ought to do a trip on those sickle-shaped erythrocytes, maybe even make 'em into discs again. **Total Bottom** had generated the idea about intimate fusing, and after that it was only a matter of Zip's stopping dancing long enough the next day in bio-lab to keep the culture dish intact as he covered it and laid it on one of the upper shelves in the backroom of the lab. He wasn't bothered that day, so he just kind of sang and thought of **The TALL One with the Pants and the Caramel Skin**. Either all the other seniors had taken study hall in the afternoon so that they could work, or the few senior girls that did come to lab always stayed in the backroom with Mr. Macintosh, the teacher, and smoked cigarettes...or something. Anyway, he'd gone to his sister's boyfriend's house as soon as he'd set the culture dish up and cleaned and put away the centrifuge. It was more of the same for Zip.

"Ohhereshegoesshereshegoes! Half the time comin' down the line she just gives you that front view 'cause she knows in America you always save the best for last. Alright, watch the turn! Here it comes! BOOM! Can anything be that big, round and firm and not sell for $2.25 off of one o'them watermelon trucks that come down from Lafayette? Oh God! I bet it's just like mama says, 'Watermelon ain't no good 'cept you eat with your hands.' Oh Bottom! Oh Mama!"

When he got to bio-lab the next afternoon, everything was exactly as it usually was: all the microscopes were covered except his, the lights were turned out, and there was smoke and giggling coming from under the backroom door. Zip didn't think anything about it. His mind was somewhere else. Hollywood to be exact.

"Yeah, Hollywood. Ain't that where they film *Soul Train?* It's somewhere out there; Hollywood, L.A., Beverly Hillbillies. Somewhere out there. Got a cousin in Inglewood. Got to call him tonight and see if he could put me up for the summer. Got an idea. Oh yeah got an idea."

He was singing a ballad as he took the culture dish off the shelf in the backroom. He never looked to his right when he went in that room because he figured people ought to be able to smoke and giggle without a person staring at them.

"Thought it wuz love, but it wuz power of course . . .."

Zip placed the culture dish on the table beside his microscope and wiped off the microscope lenses. Then he took a glass slide in his left hand while extracting from the culture with one of the disposable hypodermics that he'd pulled the cap off with his teeth.

"You tried to pull out the you in me, you baby was all you could see, all I could be/Thought it wuz love but it was power of course/Won't play this game, got to get back to the source . . . hmmm . . ."

He gently pushed out some of the culture onto the glass slide and covered it with a plastic slide, set it on the lens plate of the microscope, and looked through it with the 10x magnification on.

"Thought it wuz love, but it was power of course/All about control, got to get back to the—"

And there they were. Perfect red frisbees. And then he didn't get a chance to call his cousin in Inglewood. And then there he was in Omaha.

*   *   *

That had been five months ago. After graduation Zip had spent most of his time dodging short men with big briefcases. It had been a horrible summer. Each time he went to his sister's boyfriend's house to use the 8mm, there was some guy talking to him about his "future", and "wide open fields for minorities." Zip had never thought of himself as a minority. He'd just thought of himself as the fallen Set, flung from Hollywood, where the male angles got down all night long with **The Hair** and **Pop Dress** to the tune of "What a Fool Believes," as sung by Aretha. No, the minority that Zip smiled back at in the mirror in the morning was a different minority than the recruitment officers' inflating pupils saw as they thought of the government subsidies his genius and brown skin would bring. No, it was a noble minority that had chosen to rap in Hollywood Hills rather than serve in high school, and he had been cast out because he was smarter than the **Big Don**. "If I could redo it," he'd always mused while thinking of this fantasy. "I wouldn't tell **Big Don** that he talked too slow."

Banished from the garden though he may have been, he never stopped thinking about how to get back there. So when the most western school that wanted him had turned out to be in Omaha, he had jumped at that offer. And during the two months he'd been there he had discovered that for some reason there was no audience demand for *Soul Train* in Omaha, Nebraska, so he had to spend two-thirds of the money he got working as a lab assistant on cable tv; had made the mistake of going into a bar called "Chaps" and complained that there were no George Clinton singles on the juke box; had learned that there were no classes held on Tom Mix's birthday and that his dorm mates "didn't take kindly" to his showing up at the bio-lab that day; and had waited outside the Mutual of Omaha building every Friday since he'd arrived and not met Marlon Perkins once. It was enough to depress anyone, even Zip.

But Zip had two secrets. And, whenever he got depressed, he thought of one of them and brought that smirk back to his face; it was the same smirk he'd developed in the mirror while still in high school practicing for this line he would give to **The Tall One with the Pants and the Caramel Skin**:

"You know, baby, I been watchin you pop what you got,

so why don't we walk out on the parking lot,

I wanna put something in your ear that you gon like a whole lot;

Baby, don't you know you make me too hot!"

And then he'd do that smirk in the mirror.

And the first secret was the one that didn't really make him feel good: Zip could-n't get it right no more.

Try as he might, he couldn't make the twinkies turn into frisbees under the micro-scope. To his mind it was a very simple procedure; he followed the exact uncompli-cated steps, but no disc-shaped erythrocytes ever appeared. For a while he had thought that there was something wrong with the sickle-cell strain, but that checked out. Then he thought maybe the hypos weren't sanitized, but they checked out; the centrifuge was cleaned and inspected: it checked out also. So then he tried singing "Love TKO" to the strain, but they just lay there, unresponsive, entropic erythrocytes. The important part about this first secret is that only Zip knew it. His biology professor didn't know it, and all the other students kind of shied away from the "genius," so they weren't a problem. Everyone that was concerned just thought he was like every genius; slow, temperamental, and jerkish to the max. Well, it wasn't any of that stuff, that's what Zip wanted to tell them. He wanted friends. He wanted the truth out where everyone would know it and get off his back, and then maybe he could get the experiment right. But he couldn't tell them, because if he had told them that secret, they would have shipped him back to New Orleans before he could think of his second secret.

Zip did not want to go back to New Orleans. It was in the wrong direction. It was the southernmost Delta city of the Abyss. No. No. It had to be back to Hollywood, back to the **DonHead** or nothing. So the second secret was: Zip had decided to take flight from Omaha. He would tell no one. And he wouldn't phone his mother until **The TALL One with the Pants and the Caramel Skin** was standing over her apartment stove in his robe asking him, "How do you like your eggs, Zip honey?"

*   *   *

Only two things of any significance happened during Zip's trek from Omaha to Hollywood, and they can be related briefly here in the short, middle part of the story.

Though he pondered every waking minute about the experiment, he could not think of anything that he had recently been doing with urea, centrifuge, the hypodermic-with-the-plastic-cap, etc., that he had not done in exactly the same way in his high school bio-lab. This fact worried Zip a great deal. Suppose one of his dancers ever came down with sickle-cell? He could not have borne it. The very thought of losing **Total Bottom, Shoes-Slacks-and Legs, Pretty Face,** or **The Hair,** made him weep. He reviewed the process over and over in his head as the Greyhound rumbled west. (He had canceled the cable tv subscription and taken the return deposit to buy his one-way bus ticket to Hollywood.) The refiltering of the process yielded nothing, and he began to weep miserably over **Pretty Faces'** passing on. He could not even think of **The TALL One with the Pants and the Caramel Skin**. He became so distraught that he got off at the next stop to deposit quarters in the pay television of the terminal to search for his loves, to see that they still danced and gave to his life grace and beauty. (Yes, I wonder also why Zip could only love his six-inch-tall-nymphs from afar, and never partake of the corporeal pleasures of the backroom, smoking, and giggling with Mr. Macintosh and the senior girls. Perhaps, in keeping with his fallen Set self-concept, he found it better to view into heaven than to touch in the backroom. Who can say? It is not our place to question genius. Genius is accountable only for the marvels it produces, not the seeming incongruence of its fantasies.) He missed his bus, of course, but he eventually caught the second or third one afterwards. But at each bus terminal this touching show of human concern and total disregard for money and time was enacted. Thus, though he had left Omaha in

October, he did not get to Hollywood until December.

*   *   *

   If you could have felt as the Neanderthal felt when he found that knocking two particular types of stones together could make a shimmering, orange thing that would fight off that other thing which turned his calves and loins blue, if you could have been Buddha when he found that he never had to worry about money to see the universe because he was the universe, if you could have been Lancelot on a Friday night, with Guinevere's light on in the tower window, while Arthur was in the swamp looking for the Grail, if you could have been a French teacher in England in 1066, if you could have owned all the beachfront property at Plymouth and Jamestown around 1620, if you could have invented penicillin 1750, if you had been shrewd enough to buy up all the patent rights to those strange looking things called "machines" in 1810, if your name could have been John D. Sr., before income tax and antitrust laws, if you threw a baseball for a living and your first name were Joe and your wife's first name were Marilyn, if you could have been aware of cause and effect enough to put all your money into public condom stocks in 1979, then you would have been able to feel about half the joy and excitement that Zip felt as he stepped off that bus into Hollywood. Avoiding the twelve-year-old boy with the tight jeans and the thirty-year-old come on line, avoiding the bathroom which you never entered and returned from quite the same, avoiding the Muslim in the white-knit cap who said, "Thanks brother!" sarcastically when he did not contribute to the "Save the Children of Compton" fund drive, Zip walked out into the stinking, hot breeze of

Hollywood. There was only one thing on his mind, only one scene in his head: how to get to the studio where Soul Train was filmed.

A lady cab driver told him she knew where it was. Zip ignored her during the drive, as she continually asked him if he had any cute sisters her age. He did not even hear her as he paid his fare and she asked if she could have a naked picture of his mother.

He turned from the cab and there it was. Studio Nine seemed to do the "Tilt" in front of him, white and mosque-like. Zip danced-walked-sang toward the door, "Baby, take your time, make it shine/you can do it, baby/make all that's yours mine! Oh yes, yes." Zip howled to himself.

He pulled open the purple, metal door with the big orange letters **"DON CORNEILIUS PRODUCTIONS."** The hallway he entered was dark; at the end shone an orange light that was pulsating.

As Zip reached the end of the hallway, he stood staring at the gathered Host. He had come just before the dancing was to be video-taped, and all the dancers stood or sat in a semi-circle with their backs to him. They were listening to the **DonHead.** An overwhelming bass voice seemed to fill the room and come from every direction. Its tempo was nerve-rendingly slow. This was the **DonHead's** method of making sure that everyone listened to him. His rumbling was like a giant, old clock striking midnight: its slow drone could not be ignored; unless, of course, one were asleep, as several of the nymphs and satyrs were as the **DonHead** continued his discourse.

"Tonight's . . . taping . . . has be . . . one . . . of . . . the . . . BEST . . . you've .

. . ever . . . done." Zip knew it would be a while before the dancers could get down to business. The oracular **DonHead** always took a while as he was now 900 years old.

Zip sneaked around behind one of the big spots, but before he could get into a position to see the **DonHead** he was paralyzed. In front of him, facing the **DonHead,** with her hands on her hips, was She! **The TALL One with the Pants and the Caramel Skin** sported him a full rectal view.

"Oh God, um not gonna make it," he gasped. "Take me now, Lord. Let my eyes die with this sight on their corneas, uh, uh, uh, uhhh."

Zip held the base of one of the spotlights for support. He was dizzy. His years of television encounters had not prepared him for the undeniable authenticity of the flesh. His flesh was weak. He began to topple, knocking over the blue spot. Gratefully, everyone turned away from **DonHead** and looked at Zip. The drone ceased. **The Tall One with the Pants and the Caramel Skin** looked over her left shoulder at him with contempt.

"Not like this, please God. Don't let our first meeting be like this! We gotta get out on the parking lot . . . 'you know baby I been watching you pop what you got . . .' You remember God, please."

"What's this," he heard the **DonHead** snarl." "Boy, who you?"

"Ah, my name is Zip and I'm a famous scientist. Like, I know the cure for sickle-cell. I just dropped by to meet you and some of the dancers."

"Yeah, right," the **DonHead** said. "Nigger, please. Everybody know you homeboys come in here with your natures all on the rise, looking to cop a feel from these girls who wouldn't even cry at your funeral. Where you from boy? Misipi?"

Zip got to his feet. "Hell naw, I ain't from no 'Misipi'. I'm from New Orleans, sucker, and I have returned to Paradise. I will not be denied."

Some of the girls snickered, and one guy, whom Zip had always call 100% Natural Fluff, made a raspberry.

"Lord God, this boy is crazy! Man, somebody get this boy outta here," he heard the **DonHead** boom, and two androgenous Titans in Spandex began to move toward him.

"No. Wait a minute now," Zip shouted, "I know this looks weird, but think about my name 'Zip Roberts'. Ain't none of you never read that name nowhere?

Pretty Face spoke, "Hey, you know, I read that in *Jet* this August. This Roberts dude was supposed to be some kind of biogenius. Had a real cure for sickle-cell or cancer or something. Yeah."

The girls began to crowd around him. Zip began to sing.

"Ken, Ken where you been/

You got to meet my new friends/

6 feet 2 and self-employed/

She and her friends like all the boys."

The girls crowded closer. **Total Bottom** put her hand on his shoulder and his voiced cracked.

"You make me feel so stable/

Paying for all the food and the cable."

"Dance!" the **DonHead** shouted, and then the orange light blended with the brighter purple and red ones, and the girls took their places on the wooden loco- motive and began to lay waste to the equilibriums of the men in cable land.

Zip crawled onto the smoke stack of the locomotive and tried to get close to **The TALL one with the Pants and the Caramel Skin**, but he could barely move. He was the kid turned loose in the toy store and all the toys had come alive. The gigantic speakers screamed out Michael Henderson's "Prove It," and Zip's soul exploded. Everyone was there: **The TALL One, of course, The Hair, Total Bottom, Pretty Face, Pop Dress, Shoes- Slacks-and Legs, Solid Stuff, Lower Locomotion, Purple Tops, Little Sister, and Costumes.** And then he knew again. And the knowledge and the music and the dancers were too much. With **The TALL One** beginning to edge closer to him, with **Pretty Face** right in his face with video in full tape, Zip Roberts fainted right on the boiler, a tremendous smile on his lips.

*   *   *

When he came to, he was still smiling. His head was in the lap of **The TALL One with the Pants and the Caramel Skin,** and they were nestled alone togeth- er in a corner of the studio. And she was singing to him:

> *"Baby baby I understand/I already know you just a man./*
> *But I don't want the other girls to see/*
> *Ain't nobody in this world but you for me."*

He turned his head to look out onto the dance floor, realizing at last that the sword had been removed from the gate of Paradise and he lay nestled in nature for-ever-more. He saw **Pretty Face** doing the "Rock." In fact, everyone was rocking as the Tina Marie single got faster and faster, screaming for love. And it was then that Zip remembered that he had remembered the way to always make the accident a for-mula. He turned his head to look at **The TALL One with the Pants and the Caramel Skin,** clearing his throat, and said, *"You know, baby, I been watchin you pop what you got, so why don't we walk out on the parking lot; I wanna put some-thing in you ear that you gon like a whole lot..."* He saved the last line for the park-ing lot. She said, "Let's go right now." And she put one of his arms over her shoul-der and helped him toward the purple door.

And so he left out the rocking, endlessly cradling his missing catalyst, his X-factor. Yes, the missing link was **The TALL One with the Pants and the Caramel Skin,** herself. Or more accurately, it was the sweat that formed on Zip's fingers whenever he thought of **The TALL One** dancing, that made the accident always work, and thus change its ascription from accident to formula.

The urea, like everything else that must be helped to be at its best, had simply needed a little salt.

THIS IS NOT FICTION

"First of all, this is not fiction . . . I want to say that from the start."

* * * * * * * *

The writer paused to get himself under control. He was writing about something real, and he was trying to fight against what he felt to be intrusive emotionalism. He did not like emotionalism in himself when he wrote. It was especially important and not too difficult to remain impassive when he wrote nonfiction. Conversely, fiction was not that important, yet it was extremely difficult to handle in an appropriate, non-emotional manner. He liked emotion when he played sports and when he made love; emotion fused the two together in his mind and made each one more enjoyable. If one were emotional about everything, he reasoned, one could not appreciate the really important things when it came time. Fiction was not real life, not like nonfiction. In the weight room or on the handball court was real life. Making love was real life.

"Yes, making love. That is of importance here," he continued to write, "because J. was a homosexual, and this is what his life revolved around, and it was others' reaction to his ostentatious presentation of his sexual preference that was his ultimate undoing."

* * * * * * *

Some writers feel that good fiction is that perfect mixture of the fictional and the real, the nonfictional. H.G. Wells felt that way. Octavia Butler feels that way now. Other writers take the position that the nonfictional is unsuitable for fiction, the "real" is not real enough they claim. And they admit the difficulty of "writing" anything that is fictional with a real paper and pen. Yet they write only of the impossible, the surreal or the supernatural. Most often these writings take the shape of constructed IDEAS, as in Kafka's work ("The Metamorphosis" 1934), or in Robbe-Grillet's writings *(Les Maisons de Rendezvous,* 1966), IDEAS that have never before been made real.

* * * * * *

"Perhaps I should backtrack a bit. I want to be precise because this is not fiction. There is not room here for post-modern expansion on the truth.

Ok. I met J. in a blues club in Jackson, Mississippi in October 1977. "Charly's Angels" bounced and fluffed noiselessly from the muted monitor in the corner over the bar, and Muddy Waters' "I'm A Man" ground from the shattered cone speakers. He was working as a waiter. He also obviously liked the blues being played, and this made him immediately likeable to me. The blues are something more than music to me. In the blues, each word in every lyric is *real,* and this distinguishes this endemic United States art form from fantasy in the lyrics of music I do not love but cannot seem to live without—like Wagner's *Ring* lyrics, or those beautifully horrible cosmic lyrics, which I have so faithfully committed to memory, to be found so sketchily on any *Weather Report* jazz album.

When J. served my table, I spoke with him about the music. He was very articulate and intelligent—as well as emotional about his love of the music. Often he would talk for hours about the psychological reasons Canton, Mississippi was the only place in the world that could have produced Muddy Waters. Or he would convincingly explain why the mountains of Chattanooga can be 'heard' in the background of Bessie Smith's vibrato. He persuaded me that art was imitating life when John Lee Hooker purposely strung his guitar strings upside down in the 40's and that art imitated artifice when Jimi Hendrix did the same thing in the 60's. (He would interrupt conversations like these with intermittent discursions on the shape of male waiters' asses who happened to pass by as he exhaled cigarette smoke.) These sort of daft, speculative conversations made me like him more. (Look, a lot of parenthetical stuff is trying to intrude here, which I am not sure is really pertinent to J. and his life and the thing that happened to him later, and the difference between this piece and fiction. And it's goddamned important that I keep emotional stuff in this piece in check. Fiction is so hard to . . . to slow down. So I am going to stop this section right here—except to say that he worked with a pretty, pre-punkette looking sort of new-wave girl—S.—from a small town in Tennessee, who looked great in her jeans that had to be handpainted Spandex, even though there was very little Spandex around at that time, and who was a junkie, and who later threatened J. and me because of $300 that J. had supposedly stolen from her apartment, but it turned out that she never had $300 or an apartment. Life— any lie could become fact. Denver had even gotten into the Super Bowl. S. offered herself to me/was offered to me by J. one night, but I was too young and busy at the time, as I was 19 and working on my M.A. in English. But I will not let this emotional nonfictional material intrude on my story.)"

* * * * *

The boundaries of fiction are being expanded beyond what one would think of as boundaries of ink on paper. I hate fiction because it always ends so . . . predictably. Gordon O. Taylor wrote in an essay (*Georgia Review,* Summer, 1981) that in the past, works of fiction by Americans who were black always took as their creative center an overwhelming autobiographical element because blacks were not allowed self-hood in their real, non-fictional lives. Ishmael Reed, who is an American and also black, pushes that supportable thesis 69 steps further and puts a self in his Neo-Hoodooistic novels who is what he would like to be in his wildest, and most necessary, fantasies (see esp. *Mumbo Jumbo*, 1972) [annotation mine]. Jayne Anne Phillips (*Black Tickets* 1981) writes fiction that could not possibly be fiction because it is too ugly, too beautiful, too real. Norman Spinrad makes Hitler live to write his memoirs ("Hitler's Diaries," 1979). Maxine Hong-Kingston (*China Men*, 1982) turns the rememberable past into the metaphysical present. Albert Goldman turns hearsay into fact and fact into hearsay (I beg you not to look at the Elvis or the Lennon biographies, cause they're trash—I heard). Such things should not be possible. But these works are non-fictional. They and their authors exist.

* * * *

"So, J. and I hit it off immediately. J. seemed happy that the manager said she "would consider" playing a few of those punk songs that were so much in vogue at the club. He was also a startling dancer, in both classical and jazz forms. His limberness was not to be believed, and since his clothes were even tighter than S.'s, I could always see every muscle move as he humped and whirled and split through our living room. But god he was tremendous. While I read fiction as a professional with no time for enjoyment, J. read voraciously only for enjoyment. In fact, he only did what he enjoyed, and he enjoyed everything he did. This was another of his failings that was intricately tied to his death.

After our initial meeting, I came to the club more frequently. We attended functions together, and when my roommate—D.—decided he should move out, I immediately asked J. to move in with me. I felt we had much in common. We could go to music clubs. We could discuss literature and art. We could go dancing and drinking. Plus, I needed someone to share the rent. There was one major thing I had overlooked. (I was busy. I was young.) We did not have one thing in common."

The writer leaned back in his chair and reviewed the last few lines and spoke to himself as he wrote this sentence:

"I was not a homosexual."

* * *

It becomes very difficult to tell the real from the not-real, the fictive from the journalistic, in post-modern fiction. What one thinks is real, something with all the narrative indices of journalism, proves to be . . . something else. It is as if one made a statement that one considered to be fact, and then one was immediately presented with something tangible that cast doubt on one's belief. Thus, one has difficulty in always identifying the truth. Truman Capote wrote a book of fiction in 1979. I can't recall the name of it. Jay and I had lived together into the new spring. Then Capote appeared on *The Dick Cavett Show* and told Cavett that the book was a work of "non-fiction-fiction." Cavett had difficulty understanding this, as frankly, I did. The next day I went to a big chain bookstore, and there were five copies of Capote's book in the non-fiction section and two copies in the fiction section. The clerk assured me that the book was not misplaced. Later, she asked me what day of the week it was. She said she had forgotten. She was surrounded by calendars.

* *

"No. I was not a homosexual. And yet I could not help but reflect on this truth when I thought of how I regarded J. He was tremendous, I often thought—the way he could dance! And his body was so symmetrical. When asked to act in the world of IDEAS, there can be doubts because of the fluxal nature of the things involved. But when confronted with the physical thing, one has no doubt. One acts upon the thing. In this case, I did not act upon the thing and it was my non-action which constituted my action.

J. offered himself to me one night. He complained that he could not sleep alone and desperately needed to sleep with me. He was drunk. I told him that I slept alone or with women, and that I was not about to let him sleep with me. He continued to plead and beg. He would not stop. I was deaf. Soon he began to do this every night.

One night I had to lock my bedroom door so that I could get some sleep. The moaning, screaming, and flesh-slapping sounds from the other room were keeping me awake. I had an 8 a.m. class to teach. J. had begun to bring men home every night it seemed. He would always knock on my door, regardless of the hour, to introduce me to his bakers, dairymen, sailors, CETA workers, and Frenchmen. On this night that I had to lock my door, I drifted to sleep at some point, and at 3:30 a.m. I heard his pleading on the other side. I opened the door. One of J's front teeth was chipped and there was a slow oozing of blood from his nose.

"R," he said, "can I please come to bed with you?" And he began to cry.

Once he was in bed he stopped crying immediately. He began to joke and sing. When I told him about his face, he said, "Oh. I hadn't noticed. Really? I had no idea. Some guy just didn't like fags."

"R.," he said, "please hump me just one time. All you need is spit and determination. Everyone is bi-sexual by birth. Please. Please."

When it became obvious that I was not going to do as he asked, he began to masturbate furiously. After a short while he went to sleep with his buttocks raised in the air.

He had lost his job at the blues club a few days after moving in with me. It had gone out of business for want of a liquor license. To help ends meet, he got a part as one of the asylum inmates in Peter Weiss' Marat/Sade, but he was fired for acting too insanely. He had a car accident and began to have seizures. One night he passed out on the couch while we were talking. Mucus began to come from his nose and his eyes rolled back in his head. I cleaned him and put cold towels to his forehead until he came around. The doctors told him not to use alcohol or drugs anymore, and as a result of that advice he was drunk or high nearly all of the time during those last few weeks we lived together. He continued to come home with new men and new injuries.

One night I came home from working at my summer job at _____, a local hotel reservations chain, to find our apartment filled with people injecting liquid dexedrine into themselves. I was offered 100 valium to leave them alone. S. was among them, and she offered herself at her own suggestion this time, but I was too angry about what was going on in my apartment to realize what was going on between her and me. She offered her herself, yet she did not want me to see her shoot speed into her arm. She ran into the bathroom, locked the door, and came back a short while later. Before the rush hit her, she told me that she planned to have sex that night with one of the sons of one of Jackson's richest businessmen. The father owned a chain of barbecue places and Laundromats. She said she would profit from the deal considerably. Then she got quiet and said, 'Y'know, shit is just so unreal sometimes . . . the world. I thought if I moved to a big city like this I could make a real life for myself.' Then a car's horn honked and she was gone. I moved out the following day. J. called my parents' house and said he was crushed, that he had to live with me or he would die.

I slammed down the phone."

*

In times of great distress or change, literature responds with a moral voice in a new, adapted form. There has never been a time so filled with change as ours. And it is not just the magnitude of the changes taking place, but, as Alvin Toffler writes in

Future Shock, it is the *rate* of change which helps to make our lives so disparaging (
I think that book was written in 1972 . . .). The fiction of Loren Eiseley creates a dys-
taxy in the way we perceive the events in the story ("The Star Thrower;" I can't recall
when it was written). The story, as it were, becomes disjointed parts requiring effort
to fuss them into a coherent, ordered, whole. The writing of Jimi Hendrix distended
and metaphorized experience, so much so that once one had figured out which part
of the experience was which, one was still faced with the impossible task of making
into a workable, symbiotic whole, metaphors which bore no relation to one another
(a lot of songs could be inserted here; I can't remember the titles; the titles are not
important anyway). And yet, one still enjoyed, or labored to enjoy, the experience.
In this way, his writing was like life. It is still lifelike.

Sometimes the stress of the times, and the stress of who we are in our times,
makes it impossible for certain types of individuals to hold onto life. The great, final
too-rapid change for them becomes death. And there is nothing else but death that
will slow them and their times down. And those under that kind of stress do want
things to slow down. They *do* want things to change.

"As I visited my mother in the hospital December of 1979, J. appeared at the
door. He spoke to my mother and wished her well. He seemed more calm, more
settled. He had brought me fiction to edit. He said, 'Here's a story I wrote. It's fiction. It's about me. Edit it and I'll split the money with you when it's published.'

I took his work home and laid it in my file cabinet. In February of 1980,
when my mother had recovered to some degree, I called J. to tell him I would get to

his work as soon as possible.

His father answered the phone.

'. . . well, R, evidently you have not heard. I am sorry you have not heard. They say J. was run over by a car about 5 o'clock this morning and his skull was badly damaged. They operated on him until 7 o'clock, but, ah, J. passed away at 7:30 this morning. They say his head hit the bumper of the car . . . this is what they say any-way.'

A text for morons. Sophomoric plot development. TV melodrama worthy of something starring McClean Stevenson and Mariette Hartley. Too many essential facts missing. Stereotypical characterizations, and the worst possible, most clichéd queer-bashing ending imaginable. Had it been submitted to me for a grade I would have failed it as hopelessly trite and unbelievable. Had it been submitted to me for publication, I would have sent it back after reading the first page, the first sentence. I would have told the writer to go get some *"real"* experience before attempting to write fiction again. I would have told the writer that she/he probably would make a better grape-stomper than a writer, anything that didn't require the use of hands. Or something *real* like that I would have said—I swear to you I would have said . . . something real like that to anybody who had told me the story I just told you.

All these things I wanted to shout at J.'s father through my tears. But, instead, for a long time at my end of the phone there was a silence that I knew was real, caused by something my mind could not believe was true."

Vidnarratives

WE3

"It started like anything else I'd been involved in since I was sixteen, just a search for anything that would keep the world off my back and allow me to make money, which would allow me to have play time, which I could fill up with things and people to fit every occasion until I fell dead at 70 or so—and that's the way I click— take me or leave me, I don't give a damn." A long draw on the straw in her health shake and a look at the rain outside her bay-front window, and then StarrStarr was ready to get back to Crystal on the other end of the phone.

*   *   *

"Now, listen to this, let me talk to myself a little bit. When I lied, when I told a lie, I made three people happy; then I told the truth and three people died. What has telling the truth ever been for anybody who's honest but a pain in the ass? A lie is almost always better than the truth in matters of the heart, cause nobody really wants to hear the truth, especially me. What we rally wanna hear is the way we want to believe things are."

*   *   *

"And I remember on that day how the wind was whipping in from the Oakland Bay Bridge; and I remember that the noise in Chinatown at dusk died down to a whisper; and I remember the two of them walking toward me—Blue in his black leather, his black insulated space coat drawn tight around his waist, the collars turned up, and just that solid brown face perched on top of this mound of smooth blackness; and Billy, coming from the opposite direction, slowly walking down the hill, deliberately, his deep-blue cashmere coat barely able to contain his shoulders, his chest bursting that beautiful shirt, the thin Italian tie and that black felt hat swept at an impossible angle on his lighter-brown face, with the wisp of his soft, short curls flowing from beneath one side of the hat, his black, calf-skin covered hands clasped in front of him, hanging down toward those grey linen trousers, his black-brown eyes on Blue, Blue's light-brown eyes on him—and me, in the middle, all my terraced, moussed hair, satin dress, blue fox, and heels that made me taller than both of them, I already knew, wasted.

And me, in the middle. And them, waiting for me to say something.

And Billy, "So did you come to some kind of conclusion?"

And Blue: "So who's it gon be?'"

"Look, ah, guys, I mean, I can--we can work it out we 3!"

And Billy clearing his throat, looking down, then looking me in the eye, a tear hanging just on the rim of one of his beautiful eyes, and then him turning around and walking hurriedly back up the hill, heading east, rounding the corner.

And Blue, staring right at me, but I knew, not seeing me at all; a sigh. And then him backing up, not taking his eyes off me, then rounding the restaurant at the corner, the sun behind him blinding me, heading west.

And I sank through the sidewalk.

*   *   *

Blue remembered his two favorite vidscenes with her—and she, his love, remember, so that every time he pulled up her file on his screen, it hurt him and hurt him and hurt him, but he pulled her up over and over and over, tearing himself to pieces, and him surviving only because he enveloped her memory in a satin covering, that made her even more beautiful, even more exquisite and painful, the pain always reminding him of the difference between love and joy and the difference in danger between the two, and he loved the joy of danger—she in his pearl gray Mercedes rolling across the Oakland bridge at night, she with those long, hard, light-brown legs pouring out from beneath her blue-jean shirt and growing up into her black silk, sleeveless blouse, those hard, light-brown shoulders and round, baby eyes turned to mercilessly envelope his side image, and he trying to make reckless glances last forever and not zoom them both into the Bay, the moonlight bouncing off his amber-lighted dash and off the water and into her eyes that burned his skin.

And the memory persisting, locked in, of the day she stopped by on her lunch break, and he attacked her, exploded on her, man-handled her as softly as a rose, like Asar when he awoke and knew what Aset was, pulling her by her long fingers over to the couch, pulling her down by her shoulders, down, down, until he was standing over her on the couch, reaching down to tear open her lumber-jack shirt, to tear open her jeans, circling, sucking on her breasts as she said his name over and over as first an indicator to not make her his lunch, and second as a reminder for him to eat every crumb of her, him pulling her jeans and panties off and across the room, leaving only her green flannel shirt and tennis socks and reams and reams of woman, hard with powder and wet, and him circling and flicking and licking until her eyes rolled back in her head, not able to see him lowering and raising his clothes, putting her heels high above his head and crossing them behind his neck, and sliding into a place where hardness and softness and warmth bonded together to form one exhausted, naked, sweating body, not able to open its eyes.

But that was one life one time. And life is that thing you seldom get to rewind, that thing that replicates and mutates its own complications til you finally realize that your life is the one thing in your life that you cannot control . . . forever.

LITERARY HITMAN

All-purpose literary hit man and holder of interest the old fashioned way, known purveyor of techno-disco influenced verbiage and covert teller of truths, the last living speaker of the eradicated language of the here-and-now and the second coming of the script synclaviar, constantly at odds with the concept of a monowriter, genre limitations, depresso- and lethargiclit, confused publishing houses, anachronistic journals, and readers who judged entertainment on the thickness of the volume and whether the "good read" would last on a flight from Hannibal, MO to Portland, OR and through the Easter weekend, Larry Perry Dickerson, by day omnisexual catalyst of any writ-for-hire and by night ink-based polyglot inclined toward screenplays and flash fiction, removed his fingers from the Phoenician-lettered keyboard, inhaled, and sprang into the Atlanta dawn to face another workday. It was Monday. What would he do today?

"That was really good work you turned in the other day." The same refrain it came over and over again. It came at the end of the day from architectural firms whose letters had to be made literate. From elevator plants whose manuals had to managed into graphic language that had to clearly illustrate complex technical data on a communicational level somewhere between the first syllables a baby utters and *The Cat in the Hat Comes Back*. From the bowels of massive corporations whose animistic annual reports had to be precisely direct or indirect: direct if the rate of profit were good for the past four quarters; indirect if the managerial team had sold out the stockholders again for short term high yield, carefully covered by giving projections based on previous years' projections which were inflated in the first place. From the head minister as Larry dragged his ministerial staff kicking and screaming into pronouncing participial endings. From the law firm where three-piece suits threw briefs at him as though he were a secretary who worked for them; and when he fixed their postlapsarian Latin laxatives, they actually tried to explain to him what he had just written for them. From the editor of the medical journal who followed the "good work" comment with the addition that Larry ought to work for free because he was being exposed to a great deal of cutting- edge geriatrics knowledge. From the lover he shared with her husband who even got him to write love letters to her husband, letters so good and hot that, in 18 months, had garnered for her a diamond ring, a fur coat, and a large BMW. But at least they all paid. His lover more than most.

It all took its toll of course. At night in the Five Points stop he would scream as the car pulled into the station. "I am not a hack! I am not a pencil pusher for hire! I am a scribe for the Pentium age! Look at my hands! Ask my mama!" Then he'd go sit with the Nation of Islam guys and tell them he was a better writer than Muhammad just to piss them off. Back at his building he spat on her door each time he passed the manager's office because she'd hired him to teach resume writing to the entire building and then stolen his template and gone into the business for herself. After Cee Dee wrestled with him for an hour on purple satin sheets every Tuesday, Thursday and Saturday night, she would always force him to write another letter for her husband, never once reading one of his screen plays as he succumbed to increasing sexual indignities in an effort to bribe her to do so. "You're a ok writer baby," she'd say, poking his hairful chest with one of her long orange fingernails, "but that ain't your best talent. If I wanna read I'll go to Sunday School. See you on Tuesday". . . or Thursday or Saturday, it was all just one long awful day at the end which, he knew, god would say, "Take a letter Larry."

"Ah but today, today will be different," he thought to himself [each day]. Today I will pull out my Lotus report projections tracking all the jobs I've done for the past year and I will show each company how much better corporate communications increased their profit ratios, and then one of them, yes one of them, maybe even that snot of an old folks doctor will stake me to a year's worth of office space and some equipment money, and then I will no longer be Larry the letter writer, but Larry the Litterateur. The Modern Language Association shall hear my name and tremble."

CD Single/AFTERWORD

I will not move from Alphabet Street no matter the crime rate nor the property value.